SPELLS

A Bayou Magic Novel

KRISTEN PROBY

Ampersand Publishing, Inc.

SPELLS
A BAYOU MAGIC NOVEL

BY

KRISTEN PROBY

SPELLS

A Bayou Magic Novel

Kristen Proby

Cover Design: By Hang Le

Published by Ampersand Publishing, Inc.

Paperback ISBN: 978-1-63350-079-2

A NOTE FROM THE AUTHOR

Dear Reader,

Writing the Bayou Magic trilogy has been one of the greatest pleasures of my career so far. I adore these three sisters and the men destined to be theirs. And, I can admit, that I'm enjoying the thriller aspect of these stories very much. Although I still absolutely love writing contemporary romance, and I don't plan to stop that anytime soon, exploring paranormal romance is just downright fun.

In that spirit, what you'll read here is darker than what you'd normally expect from me. As it should be, given that we're talking about a serial killer, and a centuries-old battle. There are some edge of your seat moments, and you might find yourself wanting to cover your eyes. But hang in there, because Lucien and Millie's love story is worth every word.

I hope this second installment lives up to your expectations. Be sure to keep the lights on as you sit back with a warm beverage and let me tell you a story...

Happy reading,

Kristen

PROLOGUE

Millie

I don't like these dreams. Sometimes they're not scary, and I settle into a pleasant moment in them. But then my mind betrays me, and I'm suddenly fighting something horrible.

Something evil.

This time, it didn't start nice at all. I jumped right into the middle of a war.

Where are my sisters? Why aren't they with me?

"It's no use," I say to a woman I don't recognize. "He's too strong."

"This happens every time," she replies. How can she be so calm? Fire surrounds us, and something pulls at me. Trying to claim me. "You have to concentrate. You've been groomed for this over dozens of lifetimes."

I shake my head, frantically searching for my sisters.

"Stop, a stór mo chroí."

The male voice seems to come from inside my head. It's calm

and firm. A lifeline in the middle of all this chaos. This isn't the evil.

It could be my salvation.

I turn and see Lucien. I don't know how I know his name, but I'm certain he's Lucien, and there he is, standing at least fifty yards away. He didn't yell the word, so how did I hear him?

"Don't be afraid," Lucien says inside my head. "We'll defeat the evil one, but not today. Not yet."

"We have to!" I scream. "He's going to destroy all of us!"

I'm weakening. I feel the evil pulling, the tug stronger as if it's desperate now. Lucien starts to run toward me, but then he's gone, and I can't see him anymore.

Even the fire has disappeared.

It's just me. And him.

The evil.

I sit up in bed, sweating, my chest heaving as I gasp for air.

Brielle thinks that I have these dreams now because I hit puberty, and it's all because of hormones.

She's my older sister. She probably knows about those things.

But deep down, we both know better. We've done enough research—away from the house so Mama doesn't know—on our abilities to know that we're special. The spirits we see, the things we know, they aren't normal.

And our mama would kill us if we spoke of it in this house.

Just like she killed our daddy.

I lay back down and tug the covers up to my chin, trying to breathe normally so I can go back to sleep. Unfortunately, the spirits here know when the dreams happen, and they like to continue the torture while I'm awake.

Especially *him*. Daddy might be dead, but he's not gone.

I risk a glance into the corner of my bedroom and see him standing there. For a long time after he died, I could read his thoughts.

I had to learn how to build up my defenses because the things he thinks about are worse than any nightmare I've ever had.

I don't want to be alone. Brielle, Daphne, and I tried to talk Mama into letting us share just one bedroom, but she refused.

Mama likes to taunt us as badly as Daddy does.

We can't escape it.

Walking through the old house in the bayou in the middle of the night is its own kind of torture for me, but being with Brielle makes it worth it.

I take a deep breath, toss back the covers, and hurry from my room. I slowly open the creaky door, cringing at the sound it makes and hoping with all my might that it doesn't wake Mama.

I pause, listen, and reach out with my mind to see if she's still in bed.

She is.

And spirits surround her.

I shiver as I raise my shields again and set out down the hallway. I have to flatten myself against the wall so I don't run into one of the most aggressive ghosts we have in the house, and then I run as fast as I can down the long hallway to Brielle's room.

I close the door behind me and climb into bed with her, surprised to find our baby sister, Daphne, already there.

"We all dreamed tonight," Brielle murmurs softly as I join them. "Yours must have been bad to risk the house at night to get here."

"So much fire," Daphne whimpers. "Why is there always fire?"

"Because he's the devil," I reply and run my hand down her soft, red hair.

Suddenly, a door slams somewhere in the house.

"Oh, no," Brielle says. "Mill—"

"Already looking." I reach out again and feel everything in me go cold in terror. "Hide."

CHAPTER ONE

Millie

Early mornings at the Witches Brew are my favorite time of day. I rarely sleep. Dreams have plagued me for my entire life, and as I've gotten older, I've learned to survive on less and less rest. Instead, I use the night to learn, the early morning to enjoy, and the day to work.

The sun isn't up yet, and I'm alone here in my café in the heart of the French Quarter, adding some new potions to the menu board.

I perfected a new protection brew last week that I feel confident giving to my customers, and I tweaked the love potion just a bit.

I can't have any more men ordering that damn thing, taking a drink, and deciding I'm their soul mate. No matter how many times I tell them to wait and drink it after leaving the café, they never listen.

Men are horrible about that.

So, I had to weaken the spell a bit. Make it more of a lust potion.

Once I hang the board behind the counter, I walk to my newest addition to the space—my reading nook. I have two couches in deep purple velvet situated on opposite sides of a square coffee table—thanks to my sister Daphne's antique shop. She says the table came from a couple so deeply in love that they died within minutes of each other so one wouldn't have to know life without the other.

And Daphne would know. She's psychometric. She sees the past when she touches objects.

I fluff the colorful pillows on the couches, wipe up a ring on a side table, and make a mental note to go across the street today to buy some fresh flowers to set in front of the window that overlooks the courtyard out back.

The New Orleans French Quarter is known for its hidden courtyards, tucked back behind the shops and businesses that line the streets. I'm lucky enough to have one here. When it's not too hot outside, I open the door and offer tables and chairs for my customers to sit and enjoy the magnolia trees and the cobbled patio that connects the outside to Witches Brew.

This shop is my favorite place on Earth, and I baby it every day.

Once I have books back on their shelves , I grab a bag of garbage to take to the alley.

Brielle would yell at me for going out back by

myself in the pitch-black dark, so before I step through the door, I reach out with my mind to make sure it's safe.

No one's lurking in the shadows.

Well, no one *living*, anyway. There are plenty of spirits everywhere. But I've had my shields in place against their minds for a long, long time.

I hurry out and swing the heavy trash into the dumpster and then turn to go inside before stopping short, my senses suddenly alive in awareness.

"Meow."

I tilt my head to the side, trying to see better in the darkness. "Hi there. Excuse me."

I open the door to my shop and am surprised when the cat walks in beside me.

In the light of the café, I can see that she's a petite calico with one blue eye and one gold. She sits and wraps her long tail around her body, watching me patiently.

I already know who she is, but the eyes cement the knowledge.

"It seems I have a new familiar." I squat next to her and smile. "And aren't you beautiful?"

"Meow."

"You're welcome." I scratch her ears. "You're going to need some food, a litter box, and all kinds of fun things, aren't you?"

She rubs her face against my hand and starts to purr.

"The most important thing you need is a name.

Come on, you can help me get ready for the day, and we'll talk about it."

I walk to the dining room, the cat on my heels, and start wiping down tabletops. She jumps onto a chair and watches me.

"You have the cutest little patches of orange fur on your cheeks." I watch her as I scrub the table. "It almost looks like you're blushing."

I laugh and lean over to kiss the top of her head. When I pull back, she looks like she's smiling up at me.

This is a fun turn of events. I lost my last familiar, Luna, two years ago. And a witch doesn't choose their familiar—it's the other way around. So, I'd been waiting to see who might come into my life and when they would arrive.

"And here you are." I sit next to her, prop my chin in my hand, and talk with her. "I'm Millie, but you already know that, don't you?"

She blinks happily.

"And who are you?" My eyes keep going back to her cheeks. It really does look like she's blushing. "You know, I always had rosy cheeks, too. My high school English teacher told me they were sanguine. And I always thought that was such a pretty word. What do you think?"

She purrs again and rubs her cheek against my hand when I reach out to pet her.

"It's settled, then. Sanguine is a beautiful name for a beautiful girl. You'll stay with me at the shop today, but then you'll have to go to the house. I don't think the health inspector would be okay with me keeping a cat in a coffee shop. Don't worry, though. I'll sneak you in with me sometimes."

I walk over to the door and flick the lock, then flip the sign to *OPEN* and turn on the rest of the lights.

Sanguine jumps up onto the counter just as the bell above the door dings, signaling an incoming patron.

"You're not supposed to be up there," I hiss at her.

"Ah, she found you."

My head whips up at Lucien's voice. The man has been a part of my life for a decade, thanks to the coven I found through my mentor, Miss Sophia. But I've seen his face for far longer than that.

Lucien has been a constant in my dreams since I was a small girl. Terrifying, horrible nightmares. And because of that, I've done my best to avoid the tall, sexy warlock as much as possible.

Although, I have to admit, he was a huge help last year when my sisters and I needed it the most. For that reason alone, I'll always be grateful to Lucien.

"Good morning," I say and instinctively reach out to pet Sanguine. "How do you know my cat?"

"I've seen her around," he says and leans against the counter, grinning at us both. "She suits you."

"I'm so glad you approve." My voice is as dry as the Sahara, but Lucien doesn't even blink. It's his eyes that always get me. Ice blue and so full of wisdom, it takes a girl's breath away.

At least, it takes *mine* away. Paired with messy brown hair that's always a little overgrown, a square jawline, and hands with long, capable fingers, and Lucien is a sight to behold.

I've been drawn to him since the moment I met him.

Keeping my distance hasn't been easy. It's taken concentration, some spells, and a lot of willpower.

So I can't help feeling salty when the man walks into my business.

"It's awfully early for you to be out and about in the Quarter," I say.

"I'm headed to the lab," he says and grins when Sanguine walks right into his arms for some petting.

I'm jealous of my own familiar.

"And you want coffee?"

"Yes, please. Black is fine. And I want to talk with you."

"I'll pour, you talk." I take a disposable cup off the stack next to my machine and pour the coffee.

"Millicent, things are starting to happen."

Every damn time he says my full name, I get shivers down my spine.

"No need to be so formal," I say with a wink, trying to keep it light. "Millie's just fine. You've known me for a decade, Lucien."

"I've known you a hell of a lot longer than that," he replies. "Horace—"

"Is gone," I interrupt. "We got rid of him a year ago,

and things have been calm. There's no need to discuss this."

"Miss Sophia warned you that he wouldn't be gone forever. And you know that's true."

"*Nothing* is happening."

"Yes, it is, and I know it scares you."

"I'm not afraid of anything, because nothing is happening." But I feel my stomach tighten. In the few hours of sleep that I manage to get, I've been dreaming, and it's filled me with dread.

"You're not the only one who dreams," he says, and my eyes find his again.

"I don't know what you're talking about."

"Yes, you do."

"Stop reading my mind. I didn't give you permission to do that."

"Meow."

"You're new here," I say, pointing to Sanguine. "You don't get an opinion."

"I can't read you, and you know it," Lucien replies. "And it's damn frustrating."

I sigh and pour Lucien another cup of coffee, then toss out the one he hasn't even touched. I reach under the counter and pull up a small vial, dropping two drops into the brew.

"Are you poisoning me? Or giving me one of your famous love spells?" he asks.

"Neither." I give the coffee a quick stir and pass it over. "It's a protection potion. If you're dreaming

enough to come in here to talk to me about it, you
need it."

"I need more than this, Mill."

I shake my head, not wanting to even consider that
what he says is true. "Nothing's happening."

Lucien's ice-blue eyes narrow as he sighs and takes a
sip of his brew. "Red rose petals."

"It adds a nice flavor, I think," I reply. I've always
enjoyed talking all things magic with Lucien. He's so
damn wise. So well-versed. And I know there's so much
more I could learn from him.

But I continue keeping my distance.

"When you decide you need me, you know where to
find me."

"In a lab." Lucien is a warlock, a witch, but he also
studies blood and consults with hospitals and police
departments on many cases involving rare diseases and
DNA. He's a damn genius.

"My home, my lab, and everywhere in between. You
have my number, and I want you to use it, Millie."

"You only call me Millie when you're trying to get
on my good side."

"Millicent is a beautiful name," he murmurs and
then turns away as if he didn't just say the sweetest
thing ever. "Call me when you need me."

He leaves, and I glance down at Sanguine, who's
decided to take a bath on my counter.

"You can't do that there."

"Meow."

I T ' S   B E E N   A   D A Y . Sanguine is sweet and little and stubborn as hell. Like me. So, because she found her favorite perch on my counter, she didn't want to move. None of the customers said anything, but I didn't love it. When my employee, Esme, came in to cover the afternoon shift, I took Sanguine to the pet store to get all of her supplies and then hurried home.

"For such a little thing, you're heavy," I say as I set the cat—in her shiny new carrier—at my feet on the front porch as I search in my bag for my keys.

I literally just had them in the car. They can't have gone far.

But my bag is cavernous, and I can't find them, so I glance around to make sure no one is watching and unlock my door with a flick of my wrist.

Just a little parlor trick I picked up that comes in handy now and then.

I reach for Sanguine, and when I glance up, I frown.

"Blood on my door," I murmur. "Just a few drops."

I carry the cat inside, then return to my car for the litter and the other supplies. When I cross the threshold, I glance at the blood again.

I cleanse my home weekly. And I'm not talking about scrubbing the toilets and mopping the floor—although I do that, too. I recharge the crystals I put in all four cardinal corners, use sage, and reinforce the spell of protection that keeps out anything intent on doing me harm.

I've been much more routine about it since the Horace fiasco last year.

Over the past week, I've noticed there's been fresh blood on my door.

I don't know for sure where it's coming from or why it's there. It could be that a bird keeps hitting the door.

Suicidal bird. Poor thing.

It could be a protection spell from one of my friends.

Or, it could be Horace, trying to get inside.

I've decided not to freak out about it because I know that nothing is *inside* the house, and that's the most important thing.

"Okay, make yourself at home," I say as I open the cat carrier. I set up her litter box, food, and water dishes, and grin when I see her curled up in a happy, sunny spot on my couch. "Get some sleep for both of us, okay?"

"WHY ARE the Brussels sprouts always so dang good here?" Brielle asks as she pops another one into her mouth.

Brielle, Daphne, and I decided we needed a sister night out, and we love no restaurant in the Quarter more than Café Amalie. We've been coming here for years, specifically for the Brussels sprouts, with balsamic glaze and bacon.

They should be illegal, honestly.

"I don't know, and I don't want it to stop," Daphne says. "Okay, what's going on with you two?"

"Just work," I reply. "And it's going well. The book space in the back is a huge hit. I'm even reading tarot and runes and tea leaves back there. It's a lot of fun."

"That's awesome, Mill," Brielle says. "I've also been working a lot. It seems there will never be a time that people don't want to know about the dead haunting the New Orleans."

Brielle is a tour guide on a ghost tour here in the Quarter. It helps that she can actually *see* the shadows of the spirits that still reside here.

"And how is Cash?" I ask.

"My husband is just fine, thank you for asking."

"Do you notice that she always refers to him as her *husband*, and not by his actual given name?" Daphne asks.

"It's still new," Brielle says. "And I like calling him my husband."

"How does he like working for the NOLA PD? It has to be a huge change from the FBI," I say.

"So far, so good," she answers. "He's relieved that he doesn't have to travel as often. It wasn't a big deal when he was single, but now—"

"Now, he wants to be with you," Daphne finishes for her. "I think it's sweet. A little disgusting, but sweet."

"And how are *you*?" I ask Daphne.

"I'm fine. Business is busy for me, too, so I don't have a lot of time for anything else."

"Well, we need to do this more often," I say. "I've missed you guys. And just because I have to ask, after everything we went through last year, neither of you has started to feel anything...off, have you?"

They both frown at me. "I'm not seeing any apparitions," Brielle says. "And thank the goddess because that was the worst thing ever."

"I haven't felt anything," Daphne adds, and before I can stop her, she reaches out and touches my arm. Her eyes widen. "Oh, honey."

"What?" Brielle demands. "What is it?"

"Nothing—"

"Dreams," Daphne replies, earning a glare from me. "You need to call us when the dreams get bad like this, Mill."

"They've come and gone my whole damn life," I remind them. "They're not new."

"Lucien dropping into your shop isn't usual," Daphne replies, and I glare harder.

"You know, looking into my head is a violation, Daph."

She just smiles and takes a sip of her drink.

"Lucien came by?" Brielle asks as she swirls a sprout in the sauce on the plate, then pops it into her mouth. "Spill it. Now."

"He just wanted coffee, and to talk about shit stirring up. But *nothing* is stirred up, you guys. He's just paranoid. He needs to stay in his lab and look at DNA samples."

"Cash got to work with Lucien on a case a few months ago," Brielle says. "He was *very* impressed with Lucien's work. His analysis helped the department solve the case."

"Yeah, he's brilliant," I mutter and frown down at my plate. "Let's talk about something else."

"Why is that crowd forming?" Daphne asks, pointing out to the street. We're sitting outside in the restaurant's courtyard, and she's right, a small crowd is gathering around something in the street.

Suddenly, someone lets out a blood-curdling scream.

"Don't look, Millie," Brielle says, but she's too late. I've already reached out with my mind.

I look at them both and shake my head. "We need to go see this."

We hurry over and push our way through the crowd. In the middle of the street lies a body. A man, probably in his mid to late thirties with brown hair. He's been cut —*all* over his body.

"Some of these wounds are scabbed over," Daphne points out.

And some are fresh.

But there's no denying that he's dead. The gaping wound at his throat is a definite giveaway.

"I'm calling Cash," Brielle says.

Someone else is already talking to a 911 operator.

"Oh my goodness, what's happened?"

I turn and see my friend, Dahlia. She owns the flower shop, Black Dahlia, across the street from my café. She's also a member of my coven.

"I don't know," I reply. "But it's horrible."

"That poor man," Dahlia agrees.

We step away from the chaos as the police and ambulance arrive.

"Did you try to *see?*" Brielle asks me.

"Yeah, but I can't read anything," I reply. "I have no idea what happened to him."

"I didn't even see a shadow," Brielle adds, looking around the area. "Hey, Dahlia. How are you?"

"Well, I *was* fine," the other woman says and pushes a shaky hand through her blond hair. "I was meeting someone for dinner, but I don't think I'm hungry anymore."

"Yeah, same here," Daphne agrees. "Let's go back to the Brew and have some coffee. What do you say?"

"I think that's an excellent idea," I reply. "Dahlia, why don't you join us?"

"Oh, thanks for the invite, but I have to at least say hi to my friend. And then I have some things to do. But you three have a good night."

"Take care."

We walk away, in the opposite direction as Dahlia, and head toward my café.

"I've seen enough of this crap to last a lifetime," Brielle mumbles.

CHAPTER TWO

*"My knife's so nice and sharp I want to get to work right away
if I get a chance."*
-Jack the Ripper

Horace watches the three women walk away and finally, after all this time, feels satisfaction fill his chest. It's taken months of rest, of recovery, of *patience* to get where he is today. And it's all because of their selfishness, their *entitlement,* that he lost so much time.

How *dare* they think they could get rid of him so easily?

How could they be so ungrateful? They saw what he did for them. They know how hard he worked, for *years,* to make everything perfect. And instead of gratitude, they tried to get rid of him.

Yes, teaching them a lesson is imperative.

He smirks and turns to walk in the opposite direction, where more of his toys wait. Leaving the cup of blood in Millie's fridge last year depleted his energy. Any time he tried to manifest himself to them after that, it drained him for weeks—sometimes months.

That just wouldn't do. There was too much work to be done, too much punishment to dole out to those little bitches. He had to find another way.

Now, he realizes this is what he needed all along. Yes, this is much better.

He walks into the small house less than two miles from where he saw his girls. This dwelling was deserted after Katrina ripped through the area, leaving it uninhabitable. The front door still has the markings on it from the National Guardsmen who came through on boats, searching for survivors.

Of course, all four people who lived here were dead.

Their spirits are still here, but he's taken care of them, showed them that he's not to be messed with.

It didn't take long for him to reinforce the windows and doors and to gather some supplies. It's not nearly as good as his playroom in the bayou, but it'll have to do.

The smell of mold and feces fills the air, along with the metallic stench of fresh blood and despair.

That's what he loves the most. The despair.

He grins when he walks into the soundproofed back room and sees his two toys still tied up.

"Today was a success," he announces gleefully. "Oh, it feels so good to be back. This is important work, you see, and I'm just so relieved that it's going well already. Millie would be proud, too. She'll understand, eventually. I'll show her that all of this is for the best.

"She would *want* to be punished for all the ways she's disobeyed me."

He picks up a knife and turns toward the adjoining bathroom, approaching the tub that's already filled with water—and a toy.

"Let's get started, shall we, Lucien?"

CHAPTER THREE

Lucien

She infuriates me. She tempts me. And she worries me.

I've known since I first laid eyes on Millicent that she's afraid of the dreams we share, and of what she knows is her destiny. She's stubborn because of that fear, and reaching her won't be easy.

It never has been.

Unlike Millie, who was raised in a household of evil and terror, I grew up with a family who understood the craft, lived by it, and encouraged me to not only explore my gifts but to also prepare for the battle I was born for.

Millie didn't have that luxury, and because of that, she's working at a disadvantage. She's had to learn quicker than most, and I fear that she won't be ready in time for what we'll have to face, despite being a powerful witch.

But there's nothing I can do about that today. Until the stubborn woman is ready to listen to me and work *with* me, I have to bide my time.

Patience has become something of a work of art for me when it comes to Millicent.

It's a good thing I've had a thousand years to hone that particular skill.

Knowing that Millie's already at Witches Brew for the day, I stop by her small house to set my protection spell. I've been coming by every day for more than a week, ever since I felt the danger creeping back into our lives.

I know Millie is diligent about setting her own wards. I can feel them as I approach the door. But adding a layer of my own will intensify hers.

Our souls are linked, and because of that, anything we conjure together is much stronger than things we do alone.

After I drank her potion yesterday, I felt energized and protected in ways that I haven't since our last lifetime together.

I smile when I see Sanguine sitting in the window, watching me with her wise gaze.

No need to worry, darlin', I say to her through my mind. *I'm just here to protect you both.*

She blinks and watches as I prick my finger and wipe the few red drops that bead across the door at eye-level.

This shield is my Power to protect against evil.

This shield keeps out harm.
This shield does not allow evil or negative energies to pass.
No dark entities shall cross this barrier.
As I will it, so mote it be.

When I'm satisfied that the protection around Millie's home is strong enough for my liking, I wink at the cat and turn to walk away. Suddenly, I stop cold when the sun darkens, and I'm standing in absolute blackness. A red glow begins to burn on a foreign horizon.

It's all a mirage meant to scare me and make me distrust myself and my abilities.

But he's chosen the wrong man to fuck with.

"You're not welcome here, you evil son of a bitch."

I begin to chant, using the same words we used when we cast the circle last year. Immediately, the red glow dies, and the darkness turns back to daylight.

He's not strong enough to fight me. Not yet.

I'VE BEEN IMMERSED in the lab all morning, completely swept up in a mystery under my microscope when my phone rings.

I want it to be Millicent, but it's not. It's Cash Winslow, a member of the local police department, and husband of Millie's sister, Brielle.

"Good morning," I say when I answer the phone.

"You won't think so when I tell you why I've called," he replies

"What's up?"

"I need your help with something. We have a new vic. He was dumped in the street in front of Café Amelie last night. I'd like to run some things by you."

I narrow my eyes. "I take it something's wrong with his blood?"

"Yeah. As in, there isn't any."

"I'll be there in twenty minutes."

I hang up my lab coat and close down my lab, stowing my tools and specimens away before locking up and hurrying over to the police department.

Cash has brought me in on a few cases lately, all of them dealing with some kind of blood concern.

Blood is my job, after all. I've known since I was a small boy that working with blood would be important.

I'm lucky that I also enjoy it, find it fascinating, and it provides a good living.

When I arrive at the station, Cash is waiting for me.

"We're headed down to the morgue," he informs me. "Unless you have a problem with that."

I shake my head and walk with him to the elevator. Once in the basement, we follow a hallway to the morgue where the medical examiner is waiting.

A corpse lies on a slab in the middle of the room, the body completely covered in slashes and cuts.

"That's a shitty way to die," I say as I approach.

Some of the cuts have already formed scabs. "He was tortured."

"Mercilessly," the ME agrees. "Bled slowly for a while, and then was drained completely."

My eyes find Cash's. "Why am I here?"

"Because we also found this." Cash passes me a plastic bag containing a stone.

"It's a bloodstone," I reply, looking carefully at the smooth rock, big enough to almost fill the palm of my hand. "A big one. And it's covered, coincidentally, in blood."

"Not the victim's blood," the ME says, and my eyes shoot up to his. "The blood type on the stone, which we found in the victim's throat, doesn't match what we were able to collect from the body. And trust me, there wasn't much left."

I stare down at the rock in my hand and let myself open up to it, trying to read what happened to it before it came to be in its final resting place.

But a powerful spell has been cast on it, preventing me from seeing anything.

In fact, even trying nauseates me.

"We need an analysis on that blood," Cash insists. "I need DNA to see if it matches anyone else who might be missing. Or if I'm lucky, the killer's."

"It won't be the killer's blood," I reply without thinking.

Cash tilts his head to the side and watches me. "Why do you say that?"

"Just a hunch," I lie easily. "Can I take this with me?"

"Of course," Cash says. "I'll write you a chain of custody receipt for it."

I nod and turn away but look back at him. "Who's the vic?"

"We don't know," Cash answers with a sigh. "He doesn't match any missing persons' reports."

"Daphne might be able to help with that," I remind him. Daphne has the gift of psychometry, touching objects and people and knowing everything about it or them. I don't envy that gift.

"I'd rather not bring her in if I don't have to." Cash's face is lined with concern, and his eyes look tired.

"What aren't you telling me, Cash?"

"The girls found him." He points to the body.

I tip my head to the side. "Which girls?"

His green eyes find mine. "All three of them. He was dumped outside the restaurant where they were having dinner."

I don't like this coincidence. I don't like it at all.

"Has Brielle seen anything new since then?"

"Not that she's said."

I nod, new determination taking root in my gut.

"I'm going to drop this off at the lab and then pay Millicent a visit."

"Good luck with that."

THE BELL above her door rings as I enter the café. Her employee, Esme, is behind the counter, filling orders with a smile.

Esme is a young but powerful witch. She's also completely flighty and goofy, with messy hair and tons of jewelry draped over her wrists and neck. She's a fun addition to Witches Brew.

Millie employs mostly witches because they understand the importance of the potions added to the drinks, and because Millie doesn't have to deal with any of her employees mocking her or making fun of her.

"Hey, Lucien," Esme greets with a flirty smile. She's never made it a secret that she has a little crush on me. And I've never made it a secret that I'm not interested.

Esme isn't for me.

"Hi, Esme. Is Millie around?"

"Yeah, she's reading tarot in the back."

"Thanks." I shove my hands into my pockets and wander to her little book area, then stand and grin as I watch the woman I've loved for millennia read her cards.

"Lots of Minor Arcana Cups," Millie says, tapping the table thoughtfully. "Well, this makes sense, doesn't it?"

"How so?" the woman sitting before her asks, leaning in closer.

"Because the Cups cards always deal with emotion. You're leading with your heart instead of your head, and

that's certainly clear in every card we've drawn today
—*and* based on what you told me."

"I only told you that I was getting a divorce," the
woman says, her voice heavy with awe.

I smile wider. Yes, Millicent is damn impressive
when it comes to tarot. It's not something I ever had
any interest in, but with Millie's psychic abilities and
her flair for the dramatic, watching her read for people
is entertaining.

"You're a Cancer," Millie points out, as if that
explains it all. "You're artistic and sometimes a little
dramatic. Could it be that your decision to ask for a
divorce is based on a knee-jerk reaction to something
that hurt you?"

"I've felt so disengaged from him," the other woman
admits. "There's no *passion* anymore, you know?"

"I'm no therapist, nor an attorney, but I can tell you
based on these cards, you should have a conversation
with your husband. One that is calm and honest.
Because this indicates you're being hasty."

"Maybe I am," the client admits with a sigh. "Thank
you, Millie. You always help me so much."

"You're welcome, sugar," Millie says with a wink. She
gathers her cards and presses her hand over the deck as
the other woman leaves, whispering a little incantation
to recharge and reset them before setting them aside.

When she glances up and sees me, her brown eyes
darken. Whether in pleasure or disappointment, I'm
not sure.

"Good afternoon," I say as I approach.

"Are you here to get your cards read?" she asks.

"No." I know what my future holds. It's just how we get there that's a little hard to see. "I'd like to talk to you."

"Okay."

"Somewhere private."

Those big brown eyes narrow on me now. "I was just headed home. You can join me, if you like."

I nod, surprised by the invitation. Millie's never invited me into her home, but there's never been an occasion where I asked to speak to her privately, either.

"I'll meet you there," she says. "I just have to check in on Esme and grab my bag."

"Thanks. I mean it."

She nods, and I leave, headed for my car. The drive to Millie's house isn't a long one, and I park at the curb to wait for her to join me.

She was right. She isn't far behind me. Once she's parked in the driveway, I join her on the porch and watch as she eyes my blood mark from earlier.

She doesn't say anything, just unlocks the door with a flick of her wrist and gestures for me to follow her inside.

Sanguine comes running to greet her human, rubbing up against Millie's legs as she offers a big meow.

"Hi, darlin'," Millie says and rubs the cat's ears. Her fingers are long and strong, and I'd love to feel them on my skin.

But that's for another time.

"Whew, what a day," she chimes in before I can say anything. She leads me to her small kitchen, which has herbs hung for drying, and countertops full of pots and jars with special ingredients for her potions. "I'm having wine. Do you want some?"

I glance at the time. "It's a little early in the day for me."

"I've been awake since three," she says with a shrug as she pours half a glass of red and eyes me over the rim as she takes a sip. "Two visits in two days."

"I figured you'd be missing me by now."

I shove my hands into my pockets so I don't pull her against me and kiss the sass right out of her.

Not that I could, but I'd enjoy trying.

"Yeah, I've been heartsick all day." She takes one more sip and sets her glass aside. "Should we sit for this conversation?"

"I want to know about the body you found last night."

And just like that, all humor leaves her gorgeous face.

"How did you find out about that?"

"Cash brought me in on the investigation."

She narrows her eyes on me. "Why would he need help from a blood expert?"

"Because there's a mystery surrounding the blood," I reply. "I told you to call me if anything happened."

"Lucien,"—my heart stills at the sound of my name

on her lips—"I saw a dumped body. That's it."

"And you don't think that warrants some thought? Millie, Horace—"

"Is dead!" she yells and turns to me with angry brown eyes. "He died. We defeated him. You were there. Just because he collected blood from his victims for me doesn't mean that he's back and killing more people."

"What did you just say?"

She swears under her breath and paces around the kitchen. She's magnificent with her long, blond hair and fair skin. She's tall, almost as tall as my six feet, with a willowy body that's tempted me for as long as I can remember. And right now, I want to take her over my knee and spank her. "I didn't mean to tell you that."

"Tell me *what*?"

"Horace took trophies," she says and rubs her head in agitation, as if thinking about all of this is giving her a headache. I reach over and run my thumb over the center of her forehead, taking the pain as my own. I don't even blink as an ache settles behind my eyes.

"Thanks. Anyway, he was big into trophies, the sick piece of shit. For Brielle, it was her long, dark hair. He had dozens of braids. For Daphne, it was eyes. Because she *has the sight*, as he put it."

"And for you?" I ask, but I already know. I've always known.

"Blood." She swallows hard. "He'd saved enough blood to fill the bayou."

"And you didn't tell me."

She rounds on me, and if I were a weaker man, I'd be damn scared. "Why would I tell you, Lucien? It wasn't a detail that was released to the public, and it's not like you and I are besties. What do you expect me to do, just call you up and be like, '*Oh, hey, I know we don't speak much, but get a load of this?*'"

"Okay, fair point. So, tell me now."

She sighs. "That's really all I know. He left journals going back to when he was a teenager and first started to kill. We know he was fixated on us, and that he is most likely a psychopath."

"And he's very well-versed in dark magic," I remind her.

"*Was.* He was. Lucien, he's dead."

"You and I both know that the physical body means nothing when a being possesses powers as strong as his," I say, feeling the frustration building inside of me. "And if you think he's finished, you're wrong. Even Miss Sophia warned you that what we accomplished last year wasn't permanent."

Her lip trembles, and I feel it in my very soul. So, I reach out to her and take her hand, trying to ignore the flash of heat, the spark that ignites at the touch. "Let me help, darlin'."

"To what end?" she whispers. "You want to talk about the dreams? Fine. In every single one, no matter what time period we're in, we fail. I don't know if they're memories or a flash of what could be in the future. But every single time, it comes down to you and me, and we fucking fail, Lucien."

"Because we have in the past." She stiffens and tries to pull away, but I hold on tight. "You weren't ready to accept what you saw in those dreams, Mill. I hate that you were afraid and that you didn't have anyone to help you. To explain it to you."

"We've done this before," she whispers.

"Dozens of times," I confirm. "And he defeats us every time. But not now."

"Why is this different?"

"We're stronger. We have additional knowledge on our side. And I'm damn pissed, Millicent."

"But we don't know that this is him. First of all, Horace kills women who look like us—like me, Daphne, and Brielle. Not men. It's us sisters that he's fixated on."

"That's true," I concede. "This could have just been a sick asshole who tortured and killed that man. That case might be completely random. People are murdered in the Quarter every day."

"Exactly." She nods.

"But either way, we need to get ready. Because he won't stay dormant forever. And whether it's tonight or a year from now, we need to be prepared to deal with him again."

"I've so enjoyed the quiet this past year," she says and then turns sad eyes up to me. "What did we ever do to set all of this in motion? If it's hundreds of year's worth of a grudge, where does it come from?"

"That's one thing I don't know," I admit. "But Miss Sophia might. Or she'll know where we could look. I know you don't like me much, but we're going to be spending a bit of time together."

She scowls. "I don't *dis*like you."

"You avoid me at every turn."

She sighs and pulls out of my grasp. I let her go but feel the loss immediately.

"I've seen you since I was a child." She glances my way again. "I even knew your name. It confused and scared the hell out of me. And then, when Miss Sophia invited me to the Samhain ritual when I was seventeen and I saw you standing in that circle under the moon...it hit me like a ton of bricks. I was terrified. I recognized you, and I didn't know what to think."

"Why didn't you ask?" I brush a lock of her hair off her cheek.

"When it first started, I once tried to ask my mother about it, and she beat me with a wooden spoon until I had bloody welts on the backs of my legs."

The rage I feel is swift and encompassing.

"So I've been careful with my questions. Until I met Miss Sophia, who is always happy to answer them."

"I'm happy to answer them, too," I reply softly. "Anytime."

"Good. Because I have a feeling I'm going to have a lot of them. But the first one is pretty simple."

"Okay."

"Do you feel like lasagna for dinner?"

CHAPTER FOUR

Millie

Lucien is sitting at my kitchen island, and I'm bustling about, making us both dinner. I never thought I'd see the day.

Also, the longer I'm near him, the more I feel the chemistry between us. I know we've known each other over the course of many lifetimes, but I wonder if we were lovers in those lives, as well?

If the way he looks at me is anything to go by, or how it feels when he touches me, I'd say it's likely.

He makes me damn nervous. Which means, I can't stop talking.

"Esme asked for the entire week of Halloween off today," I say as I brown the meat in a skillet and add in some herbs and spices, along with a little something extra here and there. The noodles are already in the boiling water. "I couldn't believe it. The *whole* week, as if I don't have a festival *and* our coven ritual that week.

Which she should also be at. When I asked her why she needed the whole week off, she said it's because she wants to take the week for spiritual cleansing."

I shake my head as I dump jars of marinara into the skillet and give it a good stir.

"I would usually make my own marinara, but I'm hungry, and that's a two-day process."

"This smells fantastic," Lucien assures me. "Can you tell Esme no?"

"I did tell her no," I reply as I get to work building the lasagna in a pan. "I'm giving her a couple of days off that week, but I couldn't give her the whole week. She wasn't thrilled, but she said she understood."

"She's young," Lucien says.

"She's twenty-five," I disagree. "She's the age I was when I *opened* that shop. She's a grown woman, and she knows better."

"You're right," he replies with a nod. "Maybe she just seems younger to me. But you're right. Aside from that, how are things going at the café?"

"Really well," I reply as I sprinkle something extra-special over the lasagna's top layer before popping it into the oven. "We're consistently busy. I extended our hours on the weekends, so rather than closing at three in the afternoon, we're staying open until six. But Sunday through Thursday, we're still closing at three."

"What was that you just sprinkled on?" he asks. "Eye of newt?"

I roll my eyes and laugh as I set the pan in the hot

oven. "We don't use eye of newt anymore, Lucien. Well, not much anyway."

He raises a brow, which only makes me laugh. But now that I don't have anything to keep my hands busy with over the next forty-five minutes, I'm nervous all over again.

Bread! I can get the bread ready for the oven.

I reach for a knife and keep talking.

"How old were you when you knew you were a kitchen witch?" he asks before I can say anything else.

"I didn't know I was a witch at all until I met Miss Sophia," I reply. "Not really, anyway. I had a hunch. All I knew for sure when I was young was that I could read spirits, I saw things, and I had to learn how to build defenses around my mind so I didn't climb into random people's psyches. Reading minds is exhausting for one, and the thoughts that people have are disturbing. Not to mention, my father tormented me for over a decade after he died, and I had to escape *him*."

Lucien's blue eyes narrow on me. "How did he taunt you?"

"He stayed in that horrible house with us," I continue. "He tormented all of us, not just me. He liked to spook us, touch us. He was a horrible man. Mama was just as bad, but she was alive, so we had it coming at us from both sides."

"When did you leave?" he asks.

"Brielle turned eighteen and filed for custody of us.

Mama didn't fight it, so we went to live with Bri. I was sixteen, and Daphne was fourteen."

"That's a long time to live in a house like that," Lucien replies. His jaw is clenched, and his hand is balled into a fist on the countertop.

"It felt like an eternity," I murmur and then set the knife aside so I can pace the kitchen as I talk. "Once we moved out, and I could freely talk with others and *learn,* I started to do some research. My grandmother had given me her grimoire before she died, and I was *so* diligent at keeping it hidden from Mama and only reading it at night after she'd gone to bed.

"But one night, she found me reading it and took it away. I didn't get it back until last year. But I'd read enough to know that I gravitated to the recipes. I loved to cook, even then, and it's a good thing I did because if I hadn't, my sisters and I would have starved. Mama didn't care enough about us to feed us much."

"Lovely woman," he says with a sigh.

"Actually, after everything that happened last year, I wonder if Horace didn't put a spell on her. She was certainly possessed by *something*, but we didn't know until last year. She's been at the Psychiatric Pavilion here in New Orleans ever since. She has good days and bad ones, but it's better than living in that horrible house in the bayou."

I shake my head, thinking of my mother.

"Anyway, I'd written down many of the recipes from memory and went searching for a coven as soon as I could. That's when I found Miss Sophia. It was as if it was always meant to be."

"Because it was," he replies with a soft smile. "And when I saw you walk into our circle during that Samhain ritual you spoke of earlier, it was as if the final piece of a puzzle snapped into place. I knew you immediately. But it didn't scare me at all."

"Lucky," I murmur. "I've been scared literally all of my life, Lucien. It's exhausting."

"I hate that for you."

I don't know what to say to that, so I reach for the knife and continue slicing the bread. Suddenly, Lucien covers my hand with his.

"Why are you so nervous around me, Millicent?"

I frown, ready to deny the statement, but then I change my mind.

"Because I think you could bring a lot of chaos to my life, Lucien. And I've done my best to avoid chaos since I left that miserable house half a lifetime ago."

He cups my cheek, and the heat that stirs is undeniable.

"I'm not responsible for that chaos," he says softly as his thumb makes small circles on the apple of my cheek. "And I can bring more than that if you let me."

I sigh and lean into him. The magnetism between us is off the charts. It's a longing that I can't even begin to describe. I *want* to be near him, to care about him and have him with me. It's as if I…miss him.

Though as far as I can remember, I've never been touched by him.

But this is as familiar as it gets for me. It's as if I'm hugging my sister, as if I've done it hundreds of times.

Except I've never felt this kind of pull before, this kind of sexual energy.

Allowing myself to touch him, my hand glides up his side and over his shoulder. He turns me to face him fully and moves me so I'm flush against him, chest to knees.

"I've been waiting a long time for this." The words are almost a growl before he lowers his lips to mine. The kiss is all heat, even from the first touch. His hands plunge into my hair, and I hold on tightly, my hands anchored to his shoulders as he tastes and explores.

When he pulls back, his ice-blue eyes have darkened to a deep indigo, and he breathes hard as he stares down at me.

"Wow," I whisper and then frown. "Do you smell something burning?"

I blink rapidly, trying to clear the fog of lust from my brain, and see smoke coming out of my oven.

"Shit!"

Lucien and I work together, quickly taking the burnt lasagna from the oven and then out of the house altogether as we turn on fans and open windows.

I swirl the air, trying to get the stench out of the room.

When we've cleaned up the mess, we stare at each other for a heartbeat before dissolving into laughter.

"Well, that was a first," I say, wiping a tear from my eye. "I guess we're not having lasagna, after all."

"Sure we are," he says. "We'll go out for it."

"Good idea."

"THIS IS GOING to be *so* much fun," Mallory Boudreaux, a friend of mine, says the following day. She and I are standing out on the sidewalk in front of Witches Brew with Dahlia, making plans for our Halloween street festival that's coming up in just a couple of weeks.

With Black Dahlia just across the street from my business, and Bayou Botanicals, Mallory's shop, just a block down, we always enjoy putting our heads together to organize a fantastic French Quarter Halloween party. We're always the talk of the town.

"We'll have our standard tents set up for vendors," I say, picturing it all in my head. "And, of course, Brew will be open for cauldrons of hot chocolate."

"You should serve blood," Dahlia adds, earning weird looks from both Mallory and myself. "In the cauldrons."

"Uh...ew," Mallory says.

"Yeah, that's disgusting."

"And when the trick or treaters come through,"

Dahlia continues, "we should give every other kid an eyeball."

"What the heck is wrong with you?" Mallory asks, but Dahlia just laughs and shakes her head.

"You guys, it's *Halloween*. They make candy eyeballs, and I'm quite certain you could add something to the punch or hot chocolate to make it look like blood. Come on, get in the holiday spirit here."

"I don't want to force any kid to seek out therapy," I say, shaking my head. "So I'll pass on that. Now, we'll need at least thirty Jack-o-lanterns to line the sidewalk. I already spoke to the city, and we've been given permission to block the street to vehicle traffic. Dahlia, are you going to make black rose bouquets for the vendor tables again this year?"

"Yes, ma'am," she confirms. "I already have an extra ten dozen on order. I also bought little plastic skulls to add to the bouquets."

"Oh, I love that," Mallory says. "You know, every city should have a coven of witches plan their Halloween parties."

"No kidding," I say with a laugh. "I can't believe Halloween is only a few weeks away."

"And thank goodness we didn't plan for this festival *on* Halloween this year," Mallory agrees. "Because we have the full blue hunter's moon on All Hallows' Eve. The energy for our Samhain ritual is going to be off the charts."

"I'm so glad you decided to start practicing with us

more," I say, patting her shoulder. Mallory spent many years trying to suppress her abilities until she finally realized that she had to *use* them to finally have peace in her life. "It's so fun having you around."

"Thanks." She grins. "Okay, ladies, I'd better get back to the shop. Let me know if you need anything."

She waves and hurries down the street, and Dahlia follows me into Witches Brew.

"I know you're about to close," she says, "but I would *love* one last shot of caffeine for the day. And then I'll be out of your hair, I promise."

"Of course." I set to work making her drink just the way she likes it, and pass it over to her.

As she reaches for the cup, her sleeve falls back, revealing a nasty cut healing on her arm.

"Oh, my goddess. What happened?"

She frowns in confusion, then looks at her arm.

"Oh, that. Let's just say the thorns on roses are *nasty*. I'm always cutting myself on something.

After she pays, Dahlia waves and heads for the door.

"Have a good evening, friend!"

"You, too," I call after her. I wipe up the mess I just made and then check the time—three o'clock on the nose.

Time to close up for the day.

I turn the lock and then hurry back to the restroom before I get to work cleaning up for the evening.

When I've finished and walk to the sink to wash my hands, I take a deep breath and enjoy the smell of

Frankincense and orange that I infuse into the hand soap. I rinse and reach for a paper towel just as I glance up and see a streak of blood across the top of the mirror.

It's a *big* smudge, not like the little smears I've found on my front door recently. This one is the size of a man's hand, and it spans the entire width of the mirror.

My heart starts to pound with awareness, and the hair on the back of my neck stands on end as I lower my gaze to my reflection in the mirror.

Standing behind me, just to my right, is Horace. He's grinning like an evil Jack-o-lantern.

I spin around, but there's no one there, and then I run from the bathroom. I reach for my phone and immediately call Brielle.

"I need you here at the Brew, now. Right now. We have to cleanse this place."

"On my way. Daphne's with me. Be there in five. Are you okay?"

"No, I need you."

I hang up and pace the space behind the counter. How is this even possible?

But then I think back to what Lucien said yesterday. Was he in my house, kissing me, just yesterday? It suddenly feels like weeks ago.

He said that a physical body means nothing when a spirit possesses the powers that Horace did. *Does.*

And this means that Lucien's right.

It's starting again.

The bell above my door dings, and I glance up, expecting to see my sisters, but it's not them.

It's Lucien.

And he looks...*angry*.

"I locked that," I say as it occurs to me that Lucien just walked through a locked door.

"You're not the only one who can unlock a door with the flick of a wrist," he replies. "What's going on, Millicent?"

I start to shake my head, to deny that anything's happened, but Lucien comes around the counter and cages me between his arms.

"Don't say nothing's going on. I felt it from across town. Tell me everything."

I take a deep breath, wishing I could make this sudden headache go away. I've been getting them more frequently lately.

Lucien swipes his thumb over my forehead, and within seconds, the ache disappears.

"Stop doing that," I say softly. "I don't want you taking on my pain."

"It's what I was born to do," he says simply before leaning in to kiss my forehead. "Tell me."

I explain the blood smear on the mirror, and seeing Horace standing behind me.

"He didn't say anything," I say. "He just stood there. Grinning. Like the creep he is. I don't understand, Lucien. I cleanse this place regularly. I smudge. I have protection spells. A crystal grid. All of it."

"But you also have hundreds of energies coming in and out of here every week," he reminds me. "Hell, I've seen the little girl spirits in here for as long as I've been coming."

"Damn," I whisper. "I was hoping I'd gotten rid of them for a while."

"You can't see them?" he asks.

"No, I've built up my shields too strong," I reply. "On purpose. I don't see the spirits, but I also can't read the minds of those hundreds of energies coming in and out of here every day. It keeps me sane."

His eyes narrow on me as if he's just thought of something.

"What is it?"

"You have your shields in place."

"Yes, always."

"But Horace was able to break through and manifest to you."

I blink slowly, letting that sink in. "Well, shit."

The bell dings again, and Brielle and Daphne come hurrying inside.

"We got here as soon as we could," Brielle says and stops short when she sees Lucian. Her eyes drop to his arms, which have encircled me. "Not that it looks like you still need us."

"Of course, I do," I reply. I tell them the story I just told Lucien. "We need to cleanse this place."

"What else do we need to do?" Daphne asks. "How do we get rid of him?"

"I'm afraid that question doesn't have an easy answer," Lucien replies. "So, for now, we're going to weave some powerful spells of protection, lay some new and more powerful stones in the four corners, hang a few witch balls, and smudge the shit out of everything. And then I'm going to call Miss Sophia. It's time we had a chat."

We nod in agreement and get to work. We cast a small circle inside the shop to make sacred space for our magic, and I feel the combined strength of us wrapping around the café, keeping anything that wishes us harm out.

Nothing will be able to get in except the good energies we invite in.

After several hours of chanting and smudging, of reading my grandmother's grimoire to make sure I'm not forgetting anything, we decide to call it a day.

"I want to get home to Sanguine, just to make sure she's safe."

Lucien closes his eyes, and I can see that he's reaching out to check on my familiar.

"She's fine, but she's worried about you."

"I think it's so cool that you have a familiar again." Daphne smiles before kissing me on the cheek. "Go relax, Mil. You'll feel better in the morning."

Brielle hugs me, and then my sisters are off.

"She's right," Lucien says. "And can I just say that for two women who aren't submerged in the craft like you are, they're powerful witches in their own right?"

"Oh, they certainly are," I say with a nod. "And when it's needed, they don't hesitate to use their gifts to help me. But the craft isn't for them. Brielle uses her medium abilities for other things, and Daphne is still somewhat afraid of her Powers. But she'll learn."

"They're an important part of you," he insists. "And you'll need them."

"They won't let me down," I say. "And I know this will sound silly, but I'm not ready to be alone tonight."

"Oh, you were under the impression that I wasn't coming with you?" Lucien smirks as I lock the door behind us. "Silly witch."

CHAPTER FIVE

"I like hurting little things that can't fight back."
– Mary Bell

"It's been a wonderful day," he says, sneering in the face of one of his toys. "She *saw* me. The look of disgust in her eyes was disrespectful, so she'll have to be punished, of course. My Millicent always was the most difficult of my girls. But she'll come around."

He nods and backs away, laughing when his toy tries to free himself from his bindings.

"The new ones always struggle." Horace shakes his head with pity. "You'll learn that struggling is futile. You'll only hurt yourself, and that will anger me, Lucien. Every drop of your blood is for *me*. For Millie. And if you spill any, I'll have to punish Millie *more*. You don't want that, do you?"

The toy starts to cry, but he turns away, secretly enjoying the wailing sound of the tall, strong man.

"Now, while I'm in a good mood, I'm going to go find someone new. I had to dump that last body sooner than I thought I would, and I need a replacement."

He walks into a bedroom that holds the smell of animal feces, and steps into a black dress that shows off his host's tits well. He smears red lipstick on his pouty lips, fluffs the blond hair covering his flesh suit's head, and then walks out of the house, headed right for the bar.

He had to stop wearing heels because he just couldn't get used to walking in them, and it's easier to move around when his feet are steady under him.

He sits at the bar and orders a whiskey sour. He's never loved the taste of alcohol, but it's all part of the image—the role he's playing.

It doesn't take long before a man approaches and looks him up and down, and much to his delight, this one fits the bill just perfectly.

"Hello," the man says. "I'm Chad. What's your name?"

"Betty," he replies with a Cheshire Cat grin. "You're handsome, aren't you?"

The man blushes and looks away long enough for Horace to slip the belladonna into his drink.

Before long, the man's eyes turn glassy. The time is perfect to lead him to the playhouse.

"Come along, Lucien," he orders, wrapping an arm through his toy's. "We're going to have so much fun."

CHAPTER SIX

Millie

"We got some fantastic new books in," I inform Esme, who's just walked back to the reading nook to let me know she's here for duty.

"Some of these are paranormal romance," she says with a grin. "This is totally my jam."

"I thought you'd like them. You can borrow them, but you have to bring them back."

"I'll just come in on my day off and read back here." She flops down on the sofa and starts to read. "I love the vibe back here, Mil. It's so chill and serene."

"I think so, too." I grin as I fluff an orange pillow. "And I love that customers have been coming back here more and more to spend time. I need to add a table or two for those who want a quieter place to work on computers."

"You could put them in that corner," Esme suggests,

pointing to the room's only empty space. "Well, one at least."

"And only one because there are fire codes, and I think more than that would block the path to the doorway." I prop my hands on my hips and survey the space. "But one bistro table will do for now. Anyway, I have to run across the street to Dahlia's to pick up a fresh flower bouquet. I'll unlock the front door on my way out and flip the *OPEN* sign."

"I guess that's my cue to get my ass off this couch." She laughs and follows me out to the dining area. Esme walks behind the counter, ready to take coffee orders, and I grab the to-go cup that I already made for my friend.

"I'll be back in a few," I say as I wave and head out the door and across the street. It's way too early for Dahlia's flower shop to be open, but she's always in early and lets me come in to buy fresh blooms each morning. It always helps that I'm armed with free caffeine.

"Good morning," she says when she opens her door and holds it for me, gratefully taking her coffee. "You have no idea how badly I need this today. I'm exhausted."

"Not sleeping well?" I ask with a frown. "You know, I can give you something for that."

"Oh, it's nothing." She waves me off. "I just have times now and then when my sleep is restless. I'll rub some vetiver on my feet tonight. That should do the trick."

"Drink some chamomile tea, as well," I suggest. "And I really don't mind whipping you up a sleeping aid. I have everything I need across the street."

"I'll let you know if it comes to that," she says. "What would you like today?"

"I think I'm in a red mood," I reply after thinking it over.

"Blood red?" she asks.

"Mm, yeah. Deep red for sure. And let's add some purple to it."

She nods. "I have just the thing. Hold on."

Dahlia disappears into her large walk-in cooler, where I see her arranging flowers, choosing a stem here and there from a bucket, and then arranging some more.

When she returns, I blink rapidly at the arrangement she offers.

It's very...different for Dahlia. Bigger. Not as symmetrical as she normally does.

"Interesting," I say. "It's sort of...wild, isn't it?"

"Is it?" she looks at the flowers in my hand and then tucks a piece of hair behind her ear. "Oh, I suppose it is. It's early, and I've only had one sip of coffee. Here, I can spiff it up a bit if you like."

"No, it's fine. Thank you. Just add these to my tab."

She nods. As I turn, I hear a blood-curdling scream.

"What in the hell?" Dahlia and I both run outside, and I see a woman staring down at the bench beside the

Brew's front door, screaming as if she's being tortured to death. "What's wrong?"

The woman points, and I glance down, immediately moving the other woman back.

"What is it?" Dahlia asks.

"Call 911," I order her. "Right now."

Esme comes running outside with her phone already in hand. "On it."

"Let's get all of these people back. Sorry, folks, but I need you to stand back."

"Uh, Mil?" Dahlia says and gestures at the bench. I turn and feel my blood run cold.

It's a hand. A *severed* hand, resting on the bench, its fingers clenched in a fist. Except now, the fingers are relaxing, opening, revealing something in its palm.

"Goddess, that's gross." Esme scrunches up her nose.

"What's in there?" I murmur, bending down to get a closer look. "It looks like...a bloodstone."

"Yeah, and covered in blood," Esme says and then keeps talking to the 911 operator. "That's right, the hand is holding a stone, covered in blood."

"Don't touch it," Dahlia orders.

"I'm not." It's like I'm in a fog now, and all of the people standing around, Esme and Dahlia and all of the bystanders, feel farther and farther away. I know I shouldn't, but I *want* to touch that stone. I reach out, and as I do, the raw gem seems to light from within, shining through the thick blood surrounding it, then pulses as if it has its own heartbeat.

Just before I make contact, there's a spark, and I'm falling to the ground.

"You're under arrest, Millicent, charged with witchcraft."

I shake my head and stare into faces so familiar to me. These are my friends. This is my community. I've lived in Salem since I was born.

How can this be happening?

On one side of me stands John Anderson, pulling my left arm. On my right is my darling Lucien, also pulling me as if taking me to jail.

How could my own husband betray me like this?

I've been so careful. Never given anyone any indication that I'm anything but a Puritan, a devout Christian woman. I know that to do otherwise could be deadly, especially since young Elizabeth Hubbard and her friends started accusing women of being witches.

Women who most certainly are not.

I've seen innocents swing by their necks from trees.

And now they're taking me *away? This is lunacy.*

"I'm no witch," I say, pleading with the men to let me go. "Please, I have children to see to."

But they're not listening. The men are yelling as they drag me through the town square. But suddenly, Lucian leans in and whispers in my ear. "Stop fighting, my love. I'll get you out of this. Just trust me."

Of course, I trust him. Lucien is the love of my life, has been my husband for almost ten years. But how can he get me out of this mess? I just don't see how it's possible.

And I don't know what these men could have found to use as evidence against me.

I'm taken directly to a courtroom, where several judges sit on a platform, clearly waiting for my arrival.

"Millicent Abbott, you're charged in this court with first-degree witchcraft, which is punishable by death. How do you plead?"

"N-n-not guilty."

"Put her in a cell where she'll await trial. Next!"

Trials have been taking months. Some have died while being held.

I have children!

I'm tossed into a small cell with a dirt floor. There's a bucket in the corner. No bed. I sink to the floor and cry, full of despair.

I'm alone for what seems like hours. The shadows on the ground shift with the movement of the sun. I could open the locks with just the snap of my fingers, but that would surely give me and my abilities away, and I'd be taken to the gallows without a trial.

The moon has just risen, a full blue moon this month. It's All Hallows' Eve, and the moon is full. I'm praying fervently to the goddess to help Lucien set me free when I hear footsteps, then keys jangling. Finally, my cell door opens, and the man I love so stands in the threshold.

"You're free to go," he says. But the light has died in his eyes.

"Lucien?"

"Go home to our children, Millicent."

"Why aren't you coming with me?"

He quickly pulls me to him and kisses me hard, the embrace filled with both longing and regret. When he pulls away, he brushes his fingers through my long, blond hair.

"I love you, a stór mo chroí."

"I love you, too, my treasure. Come home with me."

"I can't." He swallows hard. "You can leave, but this is where we say goodbye. In this lifetime, at least."

"What do you speak of?"

"I turned myself in. I told them the truth, that I'm the witch in the family, and you're the innocent."

"That's not true. I'll tell them—"

"No." He grips my shoulders. "You'll say nothing, Millicent. You'll go home and tend to our children."

"I won't let you die for me." I fall into his arms, sobbing. "Please, Lucien. Please don't do this."

He kisses my head. "Don't worry, darling. We'll meet again soon, the way we've done for countless lifetimes."

More men arrive, and I'm cast aside as they take Lucien and drag him out of the building and to the gallows.

I can't let him die alone. I won't. I follow and stand in front of the angry mob, the residents holding burning torches and shouting slurs at Lucien for being a witch.

His eyes find mine.

And they don't let go until he's swinging, and the life leaves him.

The crowd cheers.

And I let out a sob turn to see to our children.

"COME ON, MILLIE." I smell the salts and open my eyes. "Ah, there she is."

"Lucien?" I glance up into his handsome face. "You got me out of jail."

He grins, but then the smile vanishes from his lips. "You passed out."

I look around, surprised to see the police already here. Cash is scowling, but he isn't looking at me.

"Oh, goddess, there's a hand." I sit up and see the extremity still sitting on the bench, undisturbed.

"Any idea how it got here?" Cash asks me.

"No. I must have walked right past it a little while ago when I went over to Dahlia's shop to get some flowers for the café. I didn't notice it."

"I didn't see it when I arrived this morning," Esme adds.

An officer is taking photos, recording the scene. The whole area around the Brew has been taped off.

Lucien helps me stand, and we back up, giving the police plenty of space to work.

Another man arrives, wearing a name badge that says *medical examiner*.

"Has the scene been processed?" he asks.

"Yeah, you can go ahead and take it." Cash gestures to the hand. "Be careful. It's holding something."

The man frowns, and then recognition dawns in his eyes when he sees the bloodstone.

"I'm fucking sick of serial killers," he mutters as he removes the hand from my bench, bags it, and takes it away.

The police finish with their questions. Shortly after, it's back to business on our little street in the French Quarter, as if there hadn't been a disembodied hand just lying about.

"Come on," Lucien says. "We're taking you home."

"Like hell, we are," I reply and step out of his reach. "I'm not sick. I'm not hurt. I *am* a little pissed off, to be honest. But I can certainly work. Besides, I'm leaving early today. Brielle, Daphne, and I are going to see Mama this afternoon."

Lucien pushes his dark-rimmed glasses up his nose and then shoves his hands into his pockets.

Why are the glasses so sexy? Because they are.

"All right, then. Call if you need me."

"How did you know this was happening?" I ask before he can turn and walk away.

"I came to see Dahlia this morning, actually." That comment bruises my ego, although the thought's completely ridiculous. "When I arrived, I saw the crowd and you reaching down to touch something that sparked. And then I had a mild heart attack when you went down. It's a bad moment that I'd rather not repeat."

Okay, ego soothed.

"Same here," I reply, my voice softer. "I'm going to have some questions for you later."

"Anytime." He winks and then turns to walk over to Dahlia's shop. The crowd has dispersed.

It's time to get back to work.

"WHAT ARE WE GOING TO DO?" Brielle asks as Daphne drives us to the hospital where Mama now lives.

"We're gonna go visit our mother," I remind her.

"No, about the other stuff. Or have you already forgotten that someone left a hand corpse at your place of business?"

"Kind of hard to forget," I murmur. "But frankly, I only have space in my brain for one uncomfortable thing at a time. Right now, it's Mama."

"She's been doing better," Daphne reminds me. "Ever since we beat Hor—"

"Don't say that name," Brielle says.

"Since he's been gone, and took whatever was controlling Mama with him, she's been much better."

"The nurse told me last time that she comes and goes," I reply. "Sometimes, she's perfectly lucid and normal. And other times, she's a little confused."

"She was possessed by evil for more than twenty years," Brielle adds. "I think all things considered, she's not doing so bad."

I nod, and Daphne parks the car. We have to check

in with a security guard, have our bags checked, and walk through a metal detector. But it isn't long before we're on our mother's floor.

"There she is," Daphne says, pointing to our mom, sitting at a table alone. She looks up when we approach, and recognition fills her eyes.

Today must be a good day.

"Well, isn't this a lovely surprise?" She smiles. It's been a shock to see her smile since she was fitted with her dentures. She looks almost pretty, which is saying a lot after the state she was in last year. "Is it visiting time again so soon? I swear, time sure does fly."

"Hi, Mama," I say and lean in to press a kiss to her cheek. She smells like peaches. "It's good to see you."

"And it's wonderful to see my girls," she says and gestures for us to sit. "It's still a bit of a shock to see you all so grown up."

Given the evil that possessed her for so long, Mama doesn't remember us growing up and moving away.

"How have you been feeling?" Brielle asks.

"Not bad, actually. I've managed to gain a few pounds, thanks to their good cookin' here. But the doctor says that's a good thing."

"I think you look lovely," Daphne says. "It's good to see you healthy, Mama."

"You know, I don't remember everything that happened over the years. None of it, really. The last thing I remember is fighting with your father and then waking up with you all grown, and Horace's house on fire."

I nod and reach out for her shaking hand. "It's okay, Mama."

"No. No, I don't s'pose it is. But I don't know what might've happened. They say here that it could be amnesia."

I share a glance with my sisters. We know it's not amnesia. Or dementia.

"Do you think that's what it was?" Brielle asks.

Mama shakes her head. "No. I think it was something much angrier than that."

"I think you're right," I say softly. "But you're free of it now. And I have to say that I'm sorry we didn't realize what was happening to you, Mama. If we'd known, we would have tried to free you from that house and the evil that had its hold on you much, much sooner."

"You didn't know," she says. "Even *I* didn't know. I've asked if I can go back to the house sometime, just so I can gather a few things. I think there are some photographs, and my mother's grimoire should be up in my bedroom."

I freeze. "What did you say?"

"My mother's grimoire," she repeats. "You know, that big book of hers? I'd like to fetch it and do some studying."

"Mama, you said it was evil. Grandma gave it to me, and you took it away. You beat us if we even suggested we might have paranormal abilities."

Mom's face goes white, and then tears fill her eyes. "I did that?"

"Yes, ma'am," Brielle says. "It's why I filed for custody of Millie and Daphne when I was eighteen, and we moved out. Because we needed help. We had questions, and you wouldn't permit it."

Mama shakes her head and covers her mouth with her hand as if she can't believe what we're telling her.

"I come from a long line of witches," she elaborates at last. "And so do you, of course. Oh, girls, there's so much I wanted to teach you, but I was waiting for you to be a little older. And then, when you were older, well..."

I blink rapidly, stunned. "You're telling me that you're a witch? That I could have learned from you all along?"

"That's right, darlin'."

I stand and pace away, so damn *angry* I could send a tornado through the room.

If innocent patients weren't sitting there, I would.

All that time, all that anguish. My own mother could have helped us. Instead, she was taken over by something so vicious, so evil that my sisters and I suffered for *years*.

"Come back," Brielle urges. She's standing next to me, her hand in mine. "Let's hear what she has to say."

"You have *got* to be kidding me, B."

"I know. I don't understand either."

I walk back to the table and sit across from Mama.

"I wish I had Miss Sophia's number," Mama says. "I know that she could help me explain everything to you."

"I have her number," I reply, a lump forming in my belly. "And trust me when I say, she's going to help you explain. I need answers."

CHAPTER SEVEN

Lucien

"Just because you're my older cousin, doesn't mean you're the boss of me," Dahlia says. She's sitting across from me in her flower shop. We just left Millie and the others, and I followed Dahlia in here.

I wanted more than anything to stay with Millicent. To make sure she's okay.

But I'm not her husband, and she has a business to run and a family to see to.

"I'm not the boss of you because I'm your cousin," I reply. "It's because you're a novitiate. My apprentice, Dahlia. You have to practice the spells and do the reading I've given you if you're going to grow in your knowledge and eventually become a permanent member of our coven. You already know this."

Dahlia's father and my father share great-grandparents. So, we aren't close cousins, but we do come from the same bloodline. Dahlia's family veered toward the darker magics, and Dahlia was raised as such.

About a year ago, she approached me and told me that the dark coven wasn't her home and hoped I'd take her on as an apprentice, to teach and guide her so she could be initiated into our coven.

She's been a fantastic and dutiful student.

Until today.

She's frowning at me, strumming her fingers on the counter. "You're quite the demanding teacher, Lucien."

"I warned you of that when we started. If it's become too much for you, say the word, and I'll use my time elsewhere."

She looks down, clenches her eyes shut, and then shakes her head. "I'm sorry. I'm so sorry. I don't mean to lash out at you. I haven't been sleeping great, and I'm just irritable. Then, seeing that awful hand on Millie's bench just threw me for a loop."

"I get it," I reply. "If today isn't a good day, we can reschedule."

"Maybe that's what I need," she agrees. "I'm sure after a few days, I'll get some rest, and I'll have time to do some studying. I'm sorry for being such a pain in the butt this week, and for wasting your time."

"I shouldn't have said that," I admit. "Just communicate with me, Dal. If you don't have time or brain space to study, let me know. It's the number of days that counts, not how quickly you can do them."

"Okay." She nods and offers me an apologetic smile.

"Thanks for being understanding. I'll make it up to you."

"Just study," I reply as I push my glasses up onto my nose and turn to walk out of her shop. It's a nice day, and I have a little while before I have to go back to the lab, so I decide to walk down a few blocks to see someone special.

I push through the glass door and smile at the man when he looks up, a loupe pressed to his eye.

"How's your day going, Dad?" I ask.

"Oh, it's a fine day, that's to be sure," he replies and takes the loupe off his head. "What are you up to?"

"I was in the Quarter this morning and thought I'd drop by."

His eyes, so like mine, narrow on me. The man has always seen right through me.

"What's troubling you?"

I blow out a breath and realize that I didn't just come down to say, "hi." I needed to talk to my father and get his advice.

"It's begun," I reply simply and watch as my father takes a deep breath and then lets it out slowly.

"We knew it would happen soon."

"I know, I'm just never ready for it."

"That's to be expected when you're dealing with evil at this magnitude," he says. "How can I help?"

"I don't know," I admit. I quickly fill him in on what I know, from the dead man with the bloodstone in his mouth, to the severed hand with the same kind of stone in its palm this morning.

"Is the blood on the stone the same as the victims' blood?"

"I haven't examined the one from this morning yet, but the first one wasn't. It's clearly from a different person. And I can't *see* where the stone came from."

"You tried?" Dad asks, his eyes wide. "You held it and dropped your shields?"

"Yes, sir. But the spell is too strong. I couldn't see anything. It made me a little sick."

"Don't do that again," Dad warns. "I know you think you're doing what needs to be done to look, to help, to solve this faster, but you're only opening yourself up to potential harm."

"I'm so frustrated," I admit and pace his shop. Dad's been a goldsmith in the Quarter since before I was born. His work is sought after all over the world. "It's never happened this way before."

"Because he's weaker than he was before."

"Yet still stronger than I'd like," I say with a sigh. "What if I can't defeat him this time?"

"You might not," Dad says and then grins when I glare at him. "I'm being a realist here, son. Stick with what you *do* know. He's weaker, but you're stronger than you've been before. And you know more. But the six   "

"Aren't together," I finish for him and drag my hand down my face. "I know."

"And until you *are*, you run the risk of losing."

"It sucks when humans with free will are stubborn."

Dad tips his head back and lets out a loud laugh. "That's for damn sure. The trick here is to be patient, Lucien."

"What if I can't be too patient? What if *he* ups the timeline on us, and there's just no time?"

"It'll all happen the way it's supposed to this time around. This part is your and Millie's journey. What happens after this isn't entirely up to you."

"I need the circle to close this time," I murmur.

"I know." He reaches out and pats my shoulder. "And for your sake, I pray to the goddess that it does."

"Thanks."

"Keep me posted. It's fascinating. And I'll ask your mother to help me dig into some more reading this evening. We may find something to help you."

"I'll take all the help I can get," I reply as a text comes in. "Looks like Cash is ready for me to take the second bloodstone."

"Looks like we'd both better get back to work."

IT'S BEEN a hell of a day.

I'm finally home, but I'm restless.

The second bloodstone has blood from the same source as the first.

It came from the same person.

What does that mean? Is the person still alive? Or is

Horace holding the blood somewhere and using it for the stones?

Of course, no one wants to say this is Horace yet. But I *know* it is. This isn't the first time he's done this.

I've just sat down at my desk with a book that I borrowed from Miss Sophia when I feel her. She didn't call or text, but Millie's on her way here.

A few seconds later, my doorbell rings.

I've lost my touch. I used to know she was coming to me before *she* did.

But we'll get there.

I open the door and smile, but then everything in me stills when I see the fury on her gorgeous face.

"What's happened?"

"Can I come in?"

I step back and gesture for her to come inside. "Of course. Tell me what's wrong."

"I'm *so mad*," she says. Her hands are in fists as she stomps around my living room. "And I can't talk to my sisters about this because they'll just try to be reasonable and defend her. And I get that. I do. But right now, I need to be angry and vent a little bit, and I don't know why, but you were the first person I thought of."

I smile as I internally dance a jig. *Finally.* "Of course, you thought of me. I'm the one you *should* vent to, sweetheart. What are we talking about?"

She blows out a breath and sits on the edge of my sofa. "My mother, the same woman who beat me with a broom handle for having the audacity to ask if the spirits I saw at night were real, or ask if there was something *different* about me. She tormented my sisters and me mercilessly."

She blows out a breath and starts to pace again.

"What did she do?" I ask.

"She's a witch," she says as she turns to me. "Now that she's clearheaded, she's talking about reading my grandmother's grimoire and studying, talking to Miss Sophia. Lucien, she's a fucking *witch*."

I want to hold her. To pull her in and soothe away this pain, because I can see that it's tearing her up inside.

But I sit on the arm of the sofa and let her rage, allow her to talk it out.

"She was possessed," I begin, but Millie turns to me, her eyes flashing.

Goddess, she's magnificent.

"No. You don't get to be the voice of reason. Because I already *know* that. But first, I get to be angry about all of the lost time. I was supposed to learn the craft from my *mother*, not be punished by her for what I am. All three of us deserved so much more than what we got. We were terrified for more than a dozen years, Lucien."

My stomach rolls at the reminder.

"I understand."

"No." She shakes her head. "You don't get it. You have parents who *helped* you learn. Who were gentle with you and kind and encouraged you to seek out your truth."

"You're right. I actually spent time with my father today, and it was exactly what I needed. I hate that you don't have that with your mother." I stand and take her shoulders in my hands. "But you can't change it, Mil. All of this anger and grief, which you're entitled to, won't change it."

She deflates and rests her forehead on my chest. "I know."

Her voice is small. I mourn for the little girl who just wanted her mother's love and guidance. Millie and her sisters needed that, and they were robbed of it.

But we're going to get justice.

I tug Millie into my arms and rub circles on her slender back. "All you can do is move forward. Defeat that piece of shit and establish a relationship with your mother from here. If that's what you want."

"What if it's not?" she asks in a small voice.

"Then you don't have to."

She lets out a shuddering breath and then looks up at me as if she just remembered something.

"You got me out of jail."

And here it is. I set her away from me, too vulnerable when it comes to this to have her touching me—at least for right now

"You said that earlier," I reply.

"Yeah." She nods and tilts her head, watching me. "I've had dreams, like I told you before, most of my life.

It's like I'm remembering something from long ago but I don't recognize anything."

"You are remembering," I say calmly. "Tell me what happened."

"When I fainted today, I had a crazy dream that I was being arrested in *Salem, Massachusetts*. I was being tried for witchcraft and put in a cell. And you were there."

Her eyes cloud over as she thinks back.

"You told me not to worry, but I was *so* worried because I was sure they'd hang me. And we had childr—"

She blushes and presses her lips together.

Yes, we had children in that life. Four. The youngest had just been born.

"Keep going."

"I was so scared and sad. Confused because I always did everything right to make sure no one suspected that I was a witch. And then you came and opened my cell and said I was free to go. But you weren't. You—"

Her lip trembles, and she has to sit on a chair. I cross to her and take her hand in mine.

"What happened to me?" I ask, but I already know.

"You gave yourself up for me. Exchanged your freedom for mine. And I watched you die."

A tear falls from her brown eye, and I catch it with my knuckle. I remember seeing her face, her beautiful brown eyes until the gallows opened, and I fell in—and then everything was black.

"But it was only a dream, right?" She looks up at me and must see the truth on my face. "That's the same look you gave me when you told me you couldn't go home with me. In 1692, Lucien."

"You were remembering a past life," I reply.

"Do you remember it?" she asks.

I bring her hand up to my lips for a kiss and then sit across from her on the coffee table. I knew we'd have this conversation sooner or later.

"Yes," I say. "But it's more complicated than that."

"Okay, explain it to me."

"You're clairvoyant," I begin, trying to describe it to her so she can understand. Not because she's not intelligent but because even I have problems understanding sometimes. "When your shields are down, you can read thoughts, spirits, that sort of thing. It's your gift."

"Yes, just like Brielle's is being a medium, and Daphne's is psychometry."

"Exactly. I'm sensitive to some of those things. I can feel spirits, and I've always sort of known things that others don't. I can reach out with my mind to see things. I guess you could say I'm a bit of a Jack of all trades when it comes to being psychic. But that's not my main gift."

She shifts in her seat. "What is?"

"I see the past, Millicent. I can remember every lifetime that you and I have spent together, down to every single detail."

She blinks and sits back but doesn't recoil.

"Has it always been that way?"

"Meaning in every lifetime?" I ask.

She nods.

"Yes. I've always had this ability."

She licks her lips and looks over my shoulder as if gathering her thoughts.

"And have I always had the same abilities?"

I smile. "Yes. And you've always been a hedgewitch."

Her lips tip up in a smile. "I like that. But I don't know that I like that you're able to remember *every* detail of our past lives, Lucien. That must be horrible."

"Not all of it is horrible. I remember each time we met and fell in love and got married. I remember our children, when they were born and how it felt to hold them. I remember making love to you. We've shared so much good over the millennia we've been linked, Millie. I'm *glad* I remember it."

"But I saw you die just one time, in a *dream*, and I couldn't bear it," she says, her eyes filling with tears again.

"And I've watched you die over and over again," I reply, running my hand over her soft hair. "And I'm going to be brutally honest here. I refuse to do it again, so we're going to kick that bastard's ass in this lifetime so I can *finally* grow old with you, Millicent."

"It seems odd that we're talking about growing old together and we haven't even been on a first date."

I laugh and then think back. "Our first date was in 998 A.D. in what is now Wales in the United Kingdom.

You were sixteen, and your father arranged with my father to marry you off to my brother. The minute I saw you, I spoke to my father—who is still my dad in this lifetime, by the way—and told him you were meant for me. So, your sire permitted me to walk with you to the village where we bought some potatoes and wheat, and we talked the whole way. We were married a month later."

"Wow, we moved fast."

I snicker. "Most people back then didn't exactly date."

She chuckles. "No, I suppose not. But we haven't had a first date in *this* lifetime, and I'm still a woman, no matter how many times I've been betrothed to you."

"That's true. I'll take you on a date this weekend, if you're free."

She smiles triumphantly. "Isn't it handy that I *am* free?"

I drag my finger down her soft cheek. "I've missed you, Millie."

"I'm sorry it's taken me so long to wake to the truth. I was just afraid. I didn't have anyone to explain things to me. Which only circles me back around to being angry at my mother."

"Rather than being angry, why don't we try this?"

I close the distance between us and brush my mouth over hers. There's no hesitation in her lips as they move beneath mine, and her hands glide over my shoulders and into my hair as I lift her from the couch, sit in her spot, and plant her on my lap.

I've waited a hundred years to have her back with me, just like this.

I cradle her cheek in my hand and settle in to enjoy her, right here, for about a decade. The way she's pressed against me, the little murmurs and moans in her throat, all of it stirs my blood. My hand drifts down from her cheek and moves over her neck to her firm breast, still covered by her purple dress.

She shifts, straddles my lap, and continues kissing me like her life depends on it.

The lights flicker.

I hear a car alarm going off outside.

But I can't stop indulging in her after being away from her for so long.

She hitches up her skirt until it bunches around her waist and then presses her center against me. Suddenly, my living room window breaks.

No, it doesn't *break*. It shatters.

We jump, and I pull Millie to me, shielding her from the glass and the horrible wind suddenly blowing through the room.

"What's happening?" she yells.

"Seems we've pissed off a dead dark witch," I reply.

CHAPTER EIGHT

"The words, 'I'm sorry' will never come out, for they would be a lie."

-- Joe "The Cannibal" Metheny

ow dare she?

Rage consumes him as he punches the wall in his little house of fun. He's been trying to teach her a lesson, and that little slut just won't listen. She's too stubborn. She's too attached to that man, and all of the visceral pleasure he brings her rather than listening to the lessons he's trying to impart.

And Horace's anger grows by the day.

"She thinks she can ignore me?" he yells as he stomps back to his new playroom and throws open the door. Three toys are shackled to the wall. The fourth, the newest one, is in the bathtub, being saved for later. Still, he stomps into the disgusting bathroom to make sure it hasn't already died of hypothermia.

That wouldn't do.

"Good," he says, his chest heaving. "This space heater is doing the trick."

"What's wrong with you, you sick piece of shit?" the toy demands, snot running from his nose as he cries. "I'm cold, and I want to go home."

"Oh, Lucien." Horace clucks his tongue and shakes his head, almost feeling pity for the toy. "Surely, you've learned by now that *I'm* in charge. I've been proving that for a millennium. I run this show, and you'll go home when I say it's time."

He tilts his head, watches the toy as he thrashes about. Horace tied his hands above his head so he couldn't try to drown himself. So although sitting naked, he's partially out of the water.

Which is why Horace brought in the space heater. He couldn't have the toy dying before his time.

"You know, maybe it's your turn today, after all."

The toys behind him moan, some in relief and others in despair. The poor toy missing a hand surely wishes he was dead. The burn on his arm where his hand used to be must hurt.

He'll let that toy live for a few more days. He deserves the pain.

The one he's had the longest is covered in cuts from where he's been bled out, almost to the point of death.

It's so interesting to see how much blood a human body can live *without* before they die.

That's a mistake Horace won't make again.

"You've angered me, Lucien," he says as he approaches the toy in the tub. "You think you can just *have* her? SHE'S MINE!"

The angry scream is shrill and right in the toy's face, the flesh now covered in his spittle and coated by his horrible breath.

"I have a plan, and you're fucking it all up. That won't do. I think it's time I teach *you* a lesson."

He reaches for his favorite knife, the one he took from a shop in the Quarter, and lets the blade glide down the man's torso but not cut.

No, not yet.

"Please," the toy whispers. "Don't do this."

"You're going to learn that you're not in control, Lucien." He tips the toy's head back, pulls out his tongue, and cuts it from the toy's head with one slash. Blood spatters the wall, covering the stains from the previous toy as screams fill the air. "Ah, yes. Yes, that's better."

CHAPTER NINE

Millie

"Oh, it feels so good to get some fresh air," Mama says from the back seat. Her window is down, and the wind blows over her smiling face. Her blond hair, streaked with very little gray, blows in the breeze.

"They let you enjoy the courtyard at the hospital, don't they?" Brielle asks from beside her.

"Oh, yes. And it's very nice, but this is better. I know the hospital is my home for now, and I quite enjoy it, but it's lovely to get out and about, too."

"Have you made friends there?" Daphne asks as she drives to the bayou so we can meet up with Miss Sophia. I was finally able to reach her yesterday after trying for almost a week. Until I made contact, I was becoming more and more frustrated, feeling like we were running out of time for some reason, though nothing specific happened to give me that impression.

I've hardly seen Lucien this week either, and that

could account for some of my moodiness. Now that I've learned more about him, I look forward to seeing him, but we've both been busy with work this week.

Tonight is our first date, and I can't wait. I just have to get through this afternoon with Mama and then I can spend some time with Lucien.

"She looks a lot like Millie."

"What?" I turn and look at Mama. "Who looks like me?"

"You always were a daydreamer," Mama says and pats my shoulder. I want to recoil at the touch. She doesn't know me well enough to know what or who I am. "I was just telling you girls about a friend I made at the hospital. She has blond hair and brown eyes like yours, and she sometimes reminds me of you. She's a sweet woman. Sad backstory, but I suppose we all have those if we live there, don't we?"

I nod and breathe a sigh of relief when Daphne pulls into Miss Sophia's driveway. Her cottage in the bayou has always been a haven for me. I've learned so much from her, spent many hours studying and talking with her. The cottage is neat with flowers and herbs planted all around the house, filling every inch of space with color and happiness.

Despite the warm fall we're having, a thin trail of smoke trails up from her chimney, signaling a fire in the hearth—most likely with something cooking there.

Miss Sophia is a modern witch, but still utilizes old-fashioned tools of the trade.

My gut tells me that she has something in her cauldron on the fire.

And I can't wait to find out what it is.

The front door opens as we all exit the car, and Miss Sophia walks out onto the porch and smiles down at us. She's a petite woman with titanium-colored hair and gray eyes, wearing jeans and a red sweater. I rarely see her dressed casually. When we're working together, she prefers to wear flowy dresses that remind me of Stevie Nicks.

The thought makes me smile.

"Good morning," Miss Sophia says as we approach the porch. "Ruth, you look lovely. It's so good to see you recovering and healthy."

Mama climbs the porch steps and enfolds Miss Sophia in a hug. "Thank you, my friend. It's been a long, long time."

"That it has. Let's go in, shall we?"

We're led inside, moving past the living room to the kitchen where there's already a pot of tea steeping, and a plate of apple muffins set out for us.

We sit at the table, and once our tea has been poured, Miss Sophia looks right at me.

"You're angry, child."

All eyes turn my way, and I shrug a shoulder. "I was angrier a few days ago. It's simmered down some. Now, I'm confused and frustrated."

"It's understandable," she replies. "This table is a place for truth, answers, and for love. It's always been that way. And, sometimes, yes, there's anger. But I won't allow that to fuel the conversation."

"Like I said, I'm okay, but I have a lot of questions."

She watches me with those shrewd eyes for a moment and then nods. "Let's see if we can't answer them then. First, Ruth, how are you doing? I'm sure you have some questions, as well."

"I don't know that you can answer them," Mama replies, her hands wrapped around her warm teacup. "I want to know where I went for all those years. I think I peeked through at times, but then it's like I was shoved aside, and I don't remember anything at all."

"First of all, I know I apologized when we found you at *his* lair, but I want to do so again." Miss Sophia takes Mama's hand in hers. "I didn't know that you'd fallen victim to him and the evil that surrounds him. If I'd known, I would have done something to stop it. Ruth, you were an angry woman in your youth, and I just thought you'd become angrier, meaner. And for those reasons, I stayed away, even after Millicent came to me and asked me to help her learn."

"I was angry," Mama admits with a nod. "My parents, although not abusive, were too involved in the coven to pay much attention to me. I loved my mother, and I miss her fiercely. I'm so glad she was good to my girls. But she had a hard time with affection. And their father was a mean man. So, no, I wasn't exactly a pleasant person to be around sometimes. And I'm sorry for that."

"No need to apologize," Miss Sophia says. "And you certainly didn't deserve to be manipulated the way you were for so long. I don't know where you were when the evil took over. I suspect you were there, observing in some way, lying dormant. As if you were asleep for a very long time. I've done some reading, and I believe that *he* put a series of spells on you, and your home, to lure evil energies there. It would make sense that he would want you incapacitated so you couldn't teach the girls about the craft. He needed them to be as defenseless as possible."

"This is so fucked up," I mutter, shaking my head. "*Why* is he so obsessed with us?"

"That goes back a thousand years," Miss Sophia answers.

"Wait." Brielle holds up a hand. "Are you saying that *he* is a thousand years old?"

"You all are, child," Miss Sophia replies. "This has been happening for many lifetimes. Though I don't know the exact reason he targeted you three. It could be you were his daughters in another life. I haven't been given that information. I only know that a war is coming that will make last year look like an amusement park, and until the six are together, he won't be defeated."

"There are only *three* of us," Daphne says.

"There will be six." Miss Sophia takes a sip of her tea. "You should all drink this. I prepared it in anticipation of what I'm sure you're going to ask of me."

We glance at each other and then at Mama, who nods. "I want to go to the house."

"No," Brielle says immediately, shaking her head. "It's not safe."

"It's toxic, and I'm not just talking about the smell," Daphne adds.

"I don't know if you're strong enough," I agree.

"I need to go." Mama's voice is strong but quiet. "I need the closure, girls. I don't want to live there again, of course. But there are a few things I'd like to gather, and I need to say goodbye."

"I think it's healthy," Miss Sophia adds. "I've put a strong protection spell on the tea, and I've asked Lucien to join us as he and I, along with Millicent, will cast a circle to protect you as you walk through the house."

I want to ask, "*Why Lucien?*." But before I can, a knock sounds on the door.

"There he is now," Miss Sophia says.

"I haven't asked all of my questions," I say.

"But you'll get all of the answers in time," she replies. "Why don't you see to the door, Millie?"

I nod and open it to find Lucien standing on the porch, dressed in jeans and a green button-down, his dark-rimmed glasses on his nose. I want to climb him like the tree of life. His lips twitch as if he can read my mind, but I know he can't. My thoughts must be written all over my face.

"Hi," I say. I sound lame even to my ears.

"Did you miss me this week?" he asks and reaches

out to brush his thumb over my forehead. "No headache?"

"No, no headache. I might have missed you a little, though. Also, this doesn't count as our date."

"Of course, not." He looks over my shoulder. "Hello, ladies."

"You're going on a date?" Daphne asks with an innocent blinking of the eyes. She's not innocent at all. "Where are you goin'?"

"I don't even know," I say and close my eyes in defeat. I didn't intend to tell my sisters about Lucien and me until later, when I could explain everything more clearly.

Looks like that plan didn't exactly pan out.

"So, are you two, like...a thing?" Brielle asks.

"We're not here to talk about Lucien and me," I remind the group, who are all grinning at me now, including the man in question. "Let's stay on task, shall we?"

"I'm Ruth," Mama says, reaching out a hand to shake his. "Are you Lucien Bergeron?"

"Yes, ma'am." He glances at me and then back at Mama in confusion. "Do you know me?"

"Well, I haven't seen you since you were a small boy, but I know your parents, of course. How are they?"

This is surreal. My mother knows Lucien and his family. Considering she didn't recognize *me* just a year ago, I don't know what to say.

"They're doing just fine, thank you, ma'am."

"Well, you let them know I said hello."

Lucien nods, and I just turn around and walk out onto the porch. "Let's do this."

Miss Sophia catches up with me and wraps her arm around my waist as we walk to the car.

"None of this is her fault, any more than it is yours, child. She didn't ask for it. Punishing her for something that isn't on her will only blacken your heart and make it easier for *him* to win."

I blow out a breath and glance back to see Lucien and my mother talking together.

"I know. I'm working on it."

"Doesn't seem to me that you are," she replies. "Maybe you need to have a conversation with her. You need to heal just as much as she does."

"I keep seeing her with that broom in her hand, beating me with it."

"It might have been her face, but it wasn't her *will* that did that. You need to think of that. And you need to set the anger aside for the next hour, or all of us could be in danger."

I nod and take another deep breath. Lucien appears by my side.

"Millie can ride over with me."

He slips his hand into mine, and I'm instantly calmer. It's as if I've just sunk down into a warm pool of water.

Miss Sophia nods, and we all climb into the two vehicles and drive toward my family's property.

"It's not pretty," I say immediately. "The house is dilapidated. It looks like something out of a horror movie, Lucien."

"Are you warning me because you're embarrassed?" He takes my hand and kisses my knuckles, which would normally unnerve me, but I'm already unsettled.

"Partly, yes. No one wants to show someone they lo —" I stop and swallow hard, shaking my head to clear it of the thought that came out of nowhere. But he heard me. "Like that their family lived like animals. It's humiliating."

"We know the why of it now, darlin'," he reminds me. "There's nothing to be embarrassed about. That doesn't concern me in the least. What worries me the most is keeping you safe, *a stór mo chroí*."

I frown over at him. "You've said that to me before. In the dreams."

He pushes his glasses up on his nose. "Have I?"

"You know you have. What does it mean?"

"It means *my heart's treasure* in Gaelic."

I blink at him, astounded. "Lucien."

He follows Daphne off the main road and down the driveway to Mama's house. "I've called you that since our first wedding day, more than a thousand years ago. And I didn't mean to say it now. It slipped out because I'm worried about this. Before you get out of this car, I want to work a spell between us, something to link us. It'll open us up to each other so you can read my thoughts and vice versa. I need to be linked to you at all times so I can protect you, and so I know you're safe."

"I've been in this place a thousand times—"

"This isn't up for discussion, Millicent."

I raise a brow, but he's not backing down. And frankly, I don't mind the extra protection. I take a moment to breathe and clear my mind, empty it of the anger and frustration from this past week, and find my center.

I feel Lucien park the car, and I can sense the energy of the house.

This horrible house.

"Boy, you weren't kidding."

I open my eyes and feel my stomach clench. The building hasn't changed much since last year. What was once a gorgeous plantation home is now nothing but a pile of ruin and rubble. The wrap-around porch has separated from the main building, and half of the roof has caved in.

I still have no idea how Mama managed to survive here for all those years.

Lucien takes my hand in his and starts to chant in a language I don't even recognize. I know he's something of a savant when it comes to the craft, but what he does takes me by surprise. The energy in the car changes, the air grows cooler, and a breeze swirls around us.

Except the windows are closed.

Suddenly, I feel a peaceful, cool calm wrap its way around me like a blanket.

This is how we'll communicate until this is over.

I hear his voice as clearly as if he spoke the words aloud. It's just like in my dreams, from the memories of previous lives.

We've been doing this for a *long* time.

I can hear you, I reply. He squeezes my hand three times and then lets go so we can climb out of the car.

"Lucien and I will stay outside and cast a spell of protection over all four of you as you journey through the house," Miss Sophia says. "That, along with the tea you drank earlier, should keep you safe. Don't dillydally. The spirits inside are sinister, and they'd love nothing more than to taunt you while you're here."

"Oh, I see them," Brielle assures her. "I thought they left with *him* when we defeated him last time."

"Some, but not all," Miss Sophia adds.

"Let's get this over with," Mama says. "The photos should be upstairs, along with the grimoire in my bedroom."

"I have the grimoire," I reply. "We came and got it last year."

"Oh." She frowns but then nods. "Good. I'm glad it's safe. Perhaps, one day, I can borrow it."

I nod and, with my sisters and I flanking her, we walk up the creaky steps to the door. Mama opens it and then gasps when she sees the state of the inside. Piles of garbage are piled in the living room. The second floor caved in entirely, and now sits in what used to be the dining room.

"Oh, this is just horrible." Mama gasps. "We worked so hard to buy this lovely house, to make it something that you girls could have for your children. And just look at it."

Brielle takes Mama's hand. "You stay with us, Mama. Promise me."

"Of course."

The spirits are everywhere, lurking in the shadows and sneering at us as we walk through. Some are livid that we're here, others seem curious.

Put your shields back up, Millicent.

I shake my head, even though Lucien can't see me. *No, I need to be able to see what's here to navigate it. I'm being careful.*

I can feel his concern and his protectiveness. I can also feel his love, and that both excites and scares me.

Both things to think about later when I'm not being attacked by the dead.

Daphne's careful not to touch anything as we make our way through the house. Everything in here is psychological torture for her, so I take her hand in mine and cast a quick spell of extra protection for her. She offers me a small smile.

"I love you," I whisper to her.

"I love you, too."

"Are these stairs passable?" Mama asks, eyeing the former grand staircase that leads to the upper floors. "I don't know if we should trust them."

"One at a time, and no one steps on the same stair.

We go single file," Brielle says. We follow her up to the second floor, thankfully without falling to our deaths.

Bonus points for us.

When we reach Mama's bedroom, I blink in surprise. It looks completely different from how it was last year when I was here to fetch the grimoire. Last year, this place was destroyed and rotting in decay.

Today, it looks as fresh and tidy as it had when we were little kids. As if Mama were here this morning to make the bed and fluff the pillows.

"I don't understand," I say.

It's an illusion, Lucien says. *It's meant to confuse you. Just keep going.*

"This place is a pit," Daphne whispers. Clearly, she and I see two very different things.

But Mama finds the table next to the bed and opens a drawer. "They're here." She pulls out two photo albums. "Just where I put them. My albums of you girls and my parents. This is what I was after."

The door slams shut behind us, locking us in.

Brielle's face turns white.

"What is it?" I ask and turn to the door, but I don't see anything.

"We need to go *now*," she replies but recoils in pain when she tries to open the door. "It's hot."

"You're not going to keep us here," I announce and hear hissing and laughter throughout the house. Suddenly, something starts to squeak in the corner.

"The rocking chair," Daphne says, pointing to the chair, which is currently moving all by itself.

It always did that.

And it's always moved to different places in the house, seemingly on its own.

You have to get out of there.

The door flies open and bangs violently against the wall.

"I want to take my mother's chair," Mama says, pointing to the rocker.

I share a look with my sisters. "That was Grandmama's chair?"

"Yes, and I want to take it. She sat there with me all those years. She protected me. I don't know how I know that, but I do. It's the only thing I remember. The chair."

"It was in your room downstairs when we came to see you last year," Brielle says. "But, Mama, I don't think we can take it with us. We don't have room."

The rocker moves faster now as if in warning.

Millicent, where are you? Come on!

"We have to go," I say and start for the door.

"The chair," Mama cries.

"We'll come back for it another time," I reply and take her hand. "Mama, we *have* to go. It's not safe for us here. Let's take the pictures and go."

Mama's crying softly with grief and fear as we hurry down the steps the way we came and head to the front door.

There's wailing and crying behind us as we step outside. Both Miss Sophia and Lucien are sweating as they chant, holding hands. They both breathe a sigh of relief when they see us.

"Did you find what you came for?" Miss Sophia asks.

"Yes, but we couldn't take my mother's chair," Mama says. "We'll have to try another time. The house was too angry, too aggressive."

Get your damn shields back up.

My eyes find Lucien's. He narrows them on me, and I immediately do as he asks, raising my protective shields so I can't read the spirits' energies anymore. My whole being calms considerably.

Thank you.

You're welcome. You're bossy, you know that?

He smiles and gives me a wink.

You can close the connection spell, I suggest. *I'm out safely.*

He nods, and I feel him quietly close the door that links us. While it's good that he can't read my mind 24/7, a piece of me immediately misses the connection.

"Is everyone okay?" Brielle asks.

"Yeah, but we need to go," Daphne says. "I hate this place."

"I'll take Miss Sophia home on my way back to town," Lucien offers.

"Thank you," I say to him, and then walk to Miss Sophia and hug her close. "Thank you, mother of my heart."

"You're welcome, daughter. Speak with Ruth. Be openminded and open-hearted so you both can heal."

"Yes, ma'am."

She and Lucien get into his car and leave, and the rest of us pile into Daphne's vehicle. She peels out of the driveway, getting us out of the bayou as quickly as possible.

"I'm so sorry, girls," Mama says. Her voice and hands are shaking. "I saw little snippets, little flashes of time while we were in there. Things that I did to you, said to you. Made you endure. And I'm horrified that you were treated that way. It's my job to protect you. I would *never* have let anyone else treat you that way, but it came from *me*. I'll never be able to forgive myself."

"Mom, it's not your fault." The words are from me. "We survived it. We're happy, productive, healthy women."

"I'm so grateful. Did you see your father?"

We're silent as we stare at Mama in the front seat. "Did *you* see him?" Brielle asks.

"I did. And he wasn't happy to see *me*."

"Mama, are you a medium?" Daphne asks.

"Of course." Mama brushes her fingers through her hair. "Before I go home, I'd like to see Millie's café, if you don't mind. Daphne, I'll have a look at your shop the next time we're out, if that's okay with you."

"Sure thing," Daphne says.

There is *so* much we need to talk about. I'll tell my sisters we need to get together tomorrow.

The rest of the ride into the city is quiet as we're all lost in thought. I breathe a sigh of relief when Daphne parks in front of Witches Brew.

This is my familiar place, my home, my safety.

We walk through it with Mama, who seems genuinely delighted by everything I've done. She sips her white chocolate mocha and sits on one of the purple sofas, looking around.

"I'm so proud of you, Millicent. This is a beautiful place, and I can see why it's a success."

"Thank you."

"I saw the potions on your board." I steel myself against the incoming criticism, but Mama just grins. "I could teach you the recipe for a little potion for healing, in case someone comes in with a headache or a sprained ankle. That sort of thing."

I blink rapidly, trying to keep the tears at bay. *This* is exactly what I've longed for all of my life.

"I'd like that. Thank you."

She nods happily and takes another look around my reading nook. "You have two little girls who hang around here, don't you?"

Brielle lets out a surprised laugh, and I can't help but join her. "Yeah, I hear I do. Brielle and Lucien see them, too."

"You don't?" Mama asks.

"No, because I have shields in place to block spirits. I inherently read their thoughts, and it's too dangerous for me."

Mama nods. "I understand. I'm glad you have your shields. Well, we should probably be going."

We walk to the front of the café, and I wave at Esme, who's manning the counter for me today.

When we step outside, I almost run right into Dahlia. "Whoa! Sorry, I didn't see you there."

"I was just coming over for an afternoon caffeine hit," she says with a laugh. "Oh, hello."

"Mama, this is Dahlia. Dahlia, this is my mom, Ruth."

Dahlia reaches out to shake Mama's hand, but Mom doesn't take it. "Are you Dahlia Bergeron?"

"That's right," Dahlia says.

"Your family was part of the dark coven."

"Yes, most still are, but that wasn't for me. I've been working with Lucien as an apprentice so I can join his coven."

"Oh. Well, how nice." Mama walks around Dahlia as if she's wary of her. "I'd like to go home now, please."

"Nice to meet you," Dahlia says with a wave, but Mama doesn't reply. She steps into Daphne's car and doesn't give us another glance as the two drive away.

"She's had a busy day," Brielle adds. "She'll need some rest tonight."

"I put a potion in her coffee," I reply. "It'll help her sleep and calm her mind."

"Good."

"Well, I'd better be off," Dahlia says and crosses the street, headed back to her shop.

"I have to go home and take a nap before my date tonight." I glance over at Brielle, who's grinning at me. "What?"

"We always knew Lucien was for you, but you were too stubborn to admit it."

"It's *one* date."

"Right."

CHAPTER TEN
Millie

"I can't believe I tried on *nine* dresses," I say as I blow out a breath and perch on the edge of my bed where Sanguine sits, watching with judgy, mismatched eyes. "I know, it's ridiculous. But it's our first date. Well, in this lifetime, anyway. And I want to look nice."

I'm in my underwear now, a matching black bra and panty set, and I've hung two of the dresses side by side so I can sit and ponder which one I like best for the occasion.

"I might not come home tonight," I inform my familiar. It's been wonderful having Sanguine with me. A witch without a familiar is a sad thing. A companion to help with magic, and I've always loved having a little friend around, Sanguine has settled in seamlessly. It's as if she's belonged here all along.

Which is exactly as it should be.

"And don't judge me about it. Oh, and if I do come

home with Lucien, don't judge me for that, either." I glance down at my cat and see her eyes narrowed. "I'm an adult woman, and if I want to have sex, I will. And something tells me that sex with Lucien will be off the damn charts."

I walk over to the dresses and choose the deep red one with the flowy sleeves and a V-neck that plunges to the center of my breasts. With this bra, my cleavage is impressive.

I slip into the silk and twirl in front of the mirror, pleased with my decision.

"The feelings I have for him are strong," I admit. "I know now that it's probably because our souls have been linked for so many years, but it was unnerving to be seventeen and, with one look, *know* that I was born to be with him. And, of course, I'm a stubborn person, so I fought it for what seems like forever. But you know what, Sanguine?"

I turn and see her watching me intently.

"I don't want to fight it anymore. It feels too good to be with him. And now we can move forward together. Because as crazy as it might sound, I'm ready to share my life with him."

I run a brush through my long hair and stare at myself in the mirror.

"And it's our first date." I can't help but laugh. "Well, no one ever accused me of being ordinary, so I guess my love life shouldn't be either."

I don't usually wear a lot of makeup, but tonight I

take my time with my eyes, giving them just a bit of a smokiness and then smooth red lipstick on my lips.

I slip my feet into black boots with a chunky heel because I have a hunch we'll be walking a bit, and heels won't work for that in or around New Orleans.

That reminds me. I need to walk down to Head Over Heels next week and ask Charly if she'd like a booth at the Halloween street party this year.

I make a mental note and then turn to Sanguine with my hands out at my sides.

"Well? What do you think?"

"Meow."

"Thank you." The doorbell rings, and butterflies immediately fill my stomach. "I don't know why I'm nervous. There's no need to be."

I grab my black shawl for when it gets cool after dark, along with my black clutch, and hurry down the steps. When I open the door, the words I was about to say die on my lips, and I can only stare at the beautiful man in front of me.

His brown hair is tamed and styled away from his face. His dark glasses frame his intense blue eyes, and his square jaw has recently been shaved.

But what his body does to the white button-down and sport coat he's wearing is most likely illegal. His legs are long and showcased in a pair of dark slacks, and I have a moment of pure female satisfaction when he takes a long perusal of me, looking from head to toe and has to swallow hard before speaking.

"You're a damn vision, Millicent."

"Thank you. You look pretty fabulous yourself." I back up so he can come inside and notice the flowers in his hand for the first time.

"These are for you."

I can't believe it. Lucien didn't bring me roses or tulips. He brought forget-me-nots.

"How did you know that these are my favorite?"

He gives me a look like *really?*

"Did you know there's an old wives' tale that says these flowers can protect people from witches?" I laugh as I carry the bouquet to the kitchen to quickly put them in some fresh water.

"Of course," he says. "They were planted all over Salem. Never affected me."

I smirk and pet a soft petal. "I love this color. It's happy. Thank you."

"You're welcome." He moves behind me and wraps his arms around my waist. He plants a kiss on my bare shoulder, right next to the silk of my dress. "This is the sexiest thing I've ever seen in all of my lifetimes."

I made the right choice. "Good." I turn to him and kiss him lightly. "That was the goal. Now, I hope you're planning to feed me, because I'm starving."

"I have a reservation at Café Amalie."

"Excellent. That's my favorite place."

"I asked Brielle where I should take you."

"At least that's one thing you don't already know about me."

"The restaurants in the Quarter were vastly different a hundred years ago," he says with a laugh, and I just stand and stare at him.

"Were we here a hundred years ago?"

His face turns serious, and he shoves his hands in his pockets. "Yes. And if you don't want me to speak of those things, I'll stop. I don't mean to scare you or make you uncomfortable. It's just nice to be able to talk about it a bit. I've never been able to before."

"It doesn't scare me," I assure him. "It's a little startling at first, but I like knowing. I want you to be able to talk to me, Lucien. Especially when it comes to matters that pertain to us. And this certainly falls into that category."

"Thank you." He leans in to kiss my forehead. "Now, as much as I'd like to keep you here all to myself and worship every inch of your body, I think we should go on our date."

"I don't mind staying in."

His smile is quick and pleased, but he just takes my hand and leads me toward the door.

"Meow."

"Don't wait up." I wink at Sanguine and follow Lucien outside. We walk down to the sidewalk, and I stop and frown. "Where's your car?"

"Right here." He points to a little Porsche convertible with the top down. It's white with a red interior and makes my mouth water. "I thought we could take this little girl out tonight."

"Jesus, Lucien," I mutter when he opens the door for me. "The blood business must pay well."

He walks around the car and sinks in next to me, then roars the engine to life.

"It doesn't do badly," he says with a wink. I hold my hair back with my hand as he takes off, and then close my eyes, enjoying the breeze as it flows over my skin. I'm an air sign and have always been able to manipulate the air around me. I love the way it feels.

As I don't live far from the Quarter, it's not long before we're parked and walking into the restaurant where we're seated in the courtyard.

"Good evening, I'm Joe, your waiter tonight."

I can't stop looking at Lucien as Joe rattles off the specials, gives us recommendations, and then leaves with our wine order, thanks to the man sitting across from me.

"Is something wrong?" he asks.

"Nope." I look down at the menu and try to get my libido under control. "I usually get the Brussels sprouts. They've managed to make a mediocre vegetable taste like candy."

"That's a must then," he agrees.

"And I'll probably do the fish special."

I close the menu and set it aside. I'm fidgety. Finally, Lucien reaches over, takes my hand, and links our fingers. I immediately calm. The current of electricity that runs between us could spark a fire, but just like earlier when we were in the car at the house in the bayou, I'm wrapped in cool calm.

"There's no need to be nervous," he says. "You're with me, and I'm the safest place you'll ever be, *a stór mo chroí*. Let's just enjoy this meal at this lovely restaurant and let me pine after you for a while."

"You say some sweet things," I say. "But by all means, pine away."

DINNER WAS DELICIOUS AND ROMANTIC. Lucien shared bites of his chicken with me, and I fed him pieces of fish. We laughed and talked about our careers and our goals there.

It was a very *normal* first-date dinner.

"Do you feel up to a walk?" I ask when we return to the car. "Not through the Quarter, but down at Audubon Park? It's a lovely evening, and I bet the old oak trees will look amazing as the sun sets."

"Of course," he says and immediately drives us six miles out of the heart of downtown to the beautiful park that is my favorite part of the city. He parks near one of the walking paths and takes my hand as we meander through the green trees that fill the huge park.

"I *love* this place," I admit as we approach a stone bridge that crosses over a river that runs through the heart of the park. "I don't take many days off, but when I do, and if I don't have a commitment with Miss

Sophia and the coven, I come here to walk and enjoy this place."

I lead him off the path to a clearing that's surrounded by ancient oak trees, their heavy limbs touching the ground.

"I like to have picnics, right here, in this spot. I've always felt drawn to it."

Lucien, who's been quiet since we arrived, takes a deep breath and then looks down at me. "Would you like to know why?"

"Sure, tell me why I'm randomly drawn to this part of a random park."

"Well, the arbor was right here," he says, pointing to a specific spot on the grass. "And the chairs were set up over there. And right where you're sitting is where we stood and exchanged vows, roughly one hundred years ago."

I feel my jaw opening and closing like a fish out of water, but I can't make my brain engage.

"Your hair was shorter then, but it was the roaring twenties, and that was the style. And your white dress was beautiful."

"We got married, right here," is all I can say.

"Yes."

I look around and feel sudden, intense sadness. My eyes fill with tears, and suddenly, Lucien's holding me, rocking me back and forth.

"I didn't mean to make you cry, darlin'."

"I wish I could remember. In all the years I've been

having the dreams, I only see the bad things. The scary stuff. I don't get to see the joy and love we shared. I feel robbed."

"I can see that," he says and kisses the top of my head. "Maybe we can figure out a way for me to show you sometime."

"The spell you conjured this morning might let me see your memories."

"It's worth looking into. But for now, let's enjoy what's happening today, Millicent."

"How long were we married?"

"Which time?"

"All of the times? How long did our marriages last? In Salem, I remember thinking that we'd been married for almost ten years."

"I think the longest was about thirty years. The shortest, a few months."

I sigh and kiss the middle of his chest before pulling back and looking up at him. "But we never parted of natural causes, in old age."

"No." He brushes his thumb over my forehead. "That's my goal in *this* lifetime."

"My stubbornness cost us some time."

"No, things are happening the way they're supposed to. You're not yet thirty. These days, that's not old to marry."

"It's a far cry from sixteen," I say with a laugh, remembering that he said I was that age the first time we met, all those centuries ago.

"Very true. I think that's a step in the right direction for feminism," he says. "By the way, do you have plans for your birthday next week?"

"How did you know—?"

He raises a brow, and I blow a raspberry through my lips.

"Our *birthdays* are always the same? My goddess, are we just living the same lives, over and over again until we get it right?"

He doesn't reply, just frowns and looks down at his shoes, and I know I've just hit the nail on the head.

"Lucien."

"I think that's the case, yes."

"Well, damn. That's heavy."

Lucien pulls me in for another hug, and we simply stand here, in this special place, breathing each other in. And it's in this moment that I decide to not waste any more time. I want to be with this man, as much and for as long as I can. He's meant for me. Just like Cash was meant for Brielle, and Jackson is meant for Daphne— although those two have some work ahead of them.

Stubborn pride has no place here.

Life is too precious.

Love is too sacred.

"I want to take you home," he murmurs. "To my home, if you'll let me."

"I thought you'd never ask."

I feel him grin against my hair, and then we walk back to the car.

Suddenly, as we approach his little white sports car, he pushes me behind him as if to protect me from something.

"Are we being mugged?" I ask and peek around his shoulder and then feel my stomach roll. A smear of blood runs along the length of the pristine vehicle. "That fucker."

"My thoughts exactly," Lucien says. "It'll wash off."

"After you collect samples and run tests, of course."

"That goes without saying, darlin'."

"Should we call Cash?"

"I'll do that on the drive home."

———

LUCIEN WAVES CASH goodbye and then leads me into the house. Cash wanted to come see the blood and take some photos, so it's been a long evening of sexual tension and frustration regarding a certain serial killer that won't go the hell away.

"He's just taunting us," I say as I slip out of my boots. "Because he's a sick son of a bitch who likes to play games."

"And as of right this instant, we're not giving him any more space in our evening," Lucien declares. As soon as we arrived, we cast a spell on the house, an extra layer of protection, just in case. "The rest of this night is just for you and me. There's no room for anyone else here."

"I like the sound of that." As he takes my hand, the lights in his old house in the Garden District house dim. "Did you do that on purpose?"

"No, I can't control electricity. Only fire, the way you control the wind and air."

"I'm an air sign, you know," I say.

"Oh, I'm aware. Our connection affects the energy around us. Electricity is energy. We might blow a fuse or two tonight."

"Fun." The laugh dies in my throat when we walk up the stairs and into his bedroom. With the snap of his fingers, at least fifty candles come to life around the room, one at a time, in a domino effect. "Wow. And, clearly, you're a fire sign. And a Sagittarius, through and through."

"How did you know I'm a Sagittarius?"

"I—" I stop and shrug. "I don't know how, or how I know that you'll be thirty-seven on November 27th, I just do."

"You remember more than you realize."

He reaches behind me and flips off the light switch, bathing us in candlelight.

"A few hundred years ago, it would have been within my rights to kill any man who looked at your skin right here," he says as he drags his fingertip down the center of my chest and into my cleavage. "And a few men at the restaurant tonight might have met that fate for as much as their eyes kept wandering over to you."

"I don't give a rat's ass about other men." I begin to

unbutton his shirt, grateful that he already shed his jacket an hour ago. My fingers aren't fumbling now, and there's no more nervousness in my body as I undress this incredible man. Our movements are slow but sure as we take our time uncovering each other as if unwrapping a precious gift.

In the flickering candlelight, Lucien guides me back onto the bed, and spends the next long moments worshipping every inch of my flesh from my lips to my toes. His touch is light and seductive, his words pure magic, and when neither of us can stand the foreplay any longer, and we finally come together, it's an explosion of emotion I've never experienced before.

The flames around us grow in intensity as Lucien takes us higher and higher, and when I reach for my climax and gasp in rapturous pleasure, the flames extinguish from the wind I've conjured.

Lucien growls and snaps his fingers, igniting the candles once more, and watches my face as he climbs closer to his own release.

Flashes of memory run through my mind. Different moments in different lifetimes, each one of us together, just like this, with the candles and the intense love we share. Both of us murmuring in languages I don't recognize, but then some I do.

He calls me *a stór mo chroí*.

And I call him *a mhuirnín*.

The flames seem to explode around us when he falls over the edge.

The candles calm to a normal, low glow, but I know I'm forever changed. I'm Lucien's, and he's mine.

"We could have set the house on fire," I murmur, still catching my breath.

"I don't think I would have cared," he says and kisses the ball of my shoulder. "I love you, *a stór mo chroí.*"

I drag my fingers down his handsome cheek. "And I love you, *a mhuirnín.*"

His eyes find mine in surprise.

"I'm remembering more," I say and brush my fingers through his hair. "Just a little bit."

And not all of it terrifies me.

CHAPTER ELEVEN

Lucien

I've always loved to watch her sleep, and it seems now is no different than before. Having Millicent in my bed is a milestone and one I've waited almost a decade for. Being patient was necessary, and I don't regret that I kept my distance and didn't push her.

But goddess above, I'm relieved that the wait is over.

I missed her more than I can say. It was an ache in my heart that never subsided.

And now she's here.

Her breaths are even, and she's safe from dreams—a little spell before she drifted off helped with that.

The sun is just rising, and the first rays of light make their way into my bedroom to chase any shadows away. I lean in to kiss her cheek and smile when she stirs and turns toward me.

"Good morning," she whispers.

"Good morning, love," I whisper in return. I pull her against me for a little cuddle and enjoy the way her long, slim body fits next to mine. "Did you sleep well?"

"Better than I have in years," she says and stretches like a lazy cat. "How about you?"

"A little." I brush her hair off her cheek. "I was in and out a bit."

"Hmm." She glances around the room and frowns. "If the sun is up, I slept longer than usual."

"It's about six," I say.

"Wow, that's late for me. Luckily, Esme's taking the morning crowd today. I don't have to go in until about noon."

"Lucky for both of us, then." I kiss her, long and slow, and let my hand drift down to cup her firm breast, teasing the already firm nipple. I'd like to stay here all morning, making love to her, but we have somewhere to be. "I should make you some coffee."

"Wow, someone making *me* coffee for a change," she says with a smile. "That's fun. But why don't we finish what you started first?"

I groan and lean in to kiss her once more but then pull away. "I would love nothing more, but I think we should meet with your sisters this morning."

She frowns. "Why?"

I don't want to say anything. Not yet. I'm not completely sure that my hunch is correct.

"It's just a feeling," I say and kiss her nose before

leaving the warm bed and stepping into a pair of lounge pants. "I'll go get that coffee."

"I'll wake up and be down in a minute."

"No hurry. I can bring the coffee here."

I leave the bedroom and shiver in the cool morning air. Autumn has firmly settled in, and the chilly mornings that come with her have arrived. I point to the fireplace in the living room as I pass, and a fire erupts in the hearth.

That'll help warm the house.

I set the first cup under the single-serve coffee maker, press brew, and turn to the back door just off the kitchen. My back yard is my oasis. I have herbs planted, along with some vegetables and flowers that have special medicinal purposes. I am not a hedgewitch, but many in our coven are, and they often ask to come and snip here and there in my garden.

It's my pleasure to share with them. I planted it all from memory, knowing that Millie would eventually need it for her practices and as a serene place to come. Perhaps one day soon, Sanguine would join her in the garden. I can picture them both, the cat lying in the grass, batting at a butterfly, and Millicent, round with child, snipping herbs for her potions.

It's real in my mind because it's as much a memory as it is a wish for what's to come.

I open the door to get some fresh air for a moment while the coffee brews, but the second I turn the knob, I know.

My hunch was right.

I glance down on the deck and sigh at the sight before me.

A foot. Severed from a body.

With a bloodstone resting on the bloody stump where it was once attached to what I assume was a man.

"Damn."

I turn back inside in time to see Millie walking into the kitchen, wearing my shirt from last night and nothing else.

Double damn.

"What's taking so long with the coffee? Do you need my help?" she asks with a sweet smile, but then she sobers when she sees my face. I'm already dialing Cash's number. "What's wrong?"

My eyes hold Millie's as I press the phone to my ear, and Cash answers. "It's Lucien. You're going to want to come over here, man. There's a foot on my back porch."

"I'll be there in twenty," the other man says and hangs up.

"No." Millie closes her eyes on a long sigh.

"I'm afraid so."

Her lip wobbles, and my gut clenches. "I was enjoying our time together, apart from the crazy."

"I know." I walk to her and wrap my arms around her, hugging her close. "I was, too. But we'll have more moments."

"I'd better get dressed." She doesn't move out of my

arms. "I wish I'd thought ahead and packed an overnight bag."

"That's something we should talk about," I begin and pull away so I can look into her face. "This is escalating, there's no doubt about it."

"A hand yesterday, a foot today." She cringes and nods. "Yeah, it's escalating."

"I'd like you to stay with me."

She narrows her eyes. "What do you mean?"

"I mean, one of us should move in with the other. I don't want you alone, Millicent. I can't protect you from across town the way I can when we're together."

She bites her lip, thinking it over. "I don't disagree. I mean, this is some creepy shit, Lucien."

"No argument."

"I guess you can come stay with me until this is all over."

My hands tighten on her shoulders, and then I let her go. "I'd rather say this is a permanent situation, but if that makes you feel better, that's fine with me. For now."

She frowns. "Wow, we're moving fast," she mutters.

"I've never moved so slowly with you in all of my lives," I reply calmly. "But this is another time, another place, and I'll go at whatever pace you want, as long as you understand that you're mine, *a stór mo chroí.*"

She tilts her head to the side. "I've known that I'm yours, and you're mine, for a very long time, Lucien. That's not being debated here."

"Good. Now, I need to examine this foot and the bloodstone on it before Cash comes and takes it away."

"Oh, I gotta see this."

"You're going to need clothes first. I don't need Cash walking up and seeing you dressed like *that*."

Her lips twitch. "Like what?"

"Like sex on a fucking platter."

"Oh good, this outfit worked, then." With that, she sashays back to the bedroom to get dressed.

I shake my head and turn back to the open door. The foot hasn't moved. Not that I expected it to. I crouch down and take a closer look.

The bloodstone is once again coated in blood, and I suspect that it's different from that of the foot. The skin on the appendage looks as if it's been burned.

"Why is it black?" Millie asks. I heard her approach from behind. She's leaning over my shoulder. "Like it's been burned."

"I was just thinking that," I murmur. "It looks like little squiggly lines."

"No, that's not it." She gets closer and suddenly reaches out a hand for the bloodstone.

"Stop." I take her hand in mine. "You can't touch it, Mill. It has a spell on it. It'll shock you again."

"It's the weirdest thing," she says, shaking her head. "It puts me in some kind of trance. I *want* to reach for it."

Fascinating. I'll have to do some research on that.

"Keep your gorgeous hands to yourself." I kiss her

knuckles and then focus back on the foot. "I wonder if that's supposed to be words."

She bends closer and then gasps. "It's the number six, Lucien. Over and over again. You know, like off an old-fashioned typewriter."

I look closer and see that she's right. "He branded it with the head of a type bar. The number six from a vintage typewriter."

She nods and sits back on her haunches. "That had to hurt."

"Probably not as badly as having the whole foot cut off," I reply just as Cash walks around the side of my house.

"Please tell me neither of you touched it."

"Ew, no," Millie says. "You know me better than that, brother-in-law."

"At least this time you aren't unconscious." Cash looks down at the foot. "Christ Jesus."

"So, Lucien found a foot," Millie says, gesturing dramatically. "As you can see."

"Are you always a smartass in the morning?" Cash asks.

"Yes," we both say at once. Millie raises a brow at me, and I just shrug.

"Tell the ME to pay extra attention to the brandings on the skin," I suggest to Cash.

"Brandings?" he asks and takes a closer look. "Fuck, it's tiny sixes all over."

"That's what I see."

"What else do you see?" he asks. Cash is married to Brielle and has been a part of this since the beginning when Horace started making himself known to Brielle last year. I know I can be brutally honest with the other man about what I see, either with my eyes, or my mind.

"Not enough," I reply in frustration. "I'm only picking up on impressions here and there. An urgency. I think he's only going to escalate from here. We need a meeting with all three sisters this morning."

"Agreed," Cash says. "Just when I thought the spooky, psycho shit was done for a while, here we are. The ME's on his way over now. I'm going to record the scene, and then we'll be out of your hair."

"I'll call my sisters," Millie interjects.

"Looks like we're having a family meeting today," Cash says. "I wish it was about something happy. Like Christmas."

"Me, too," Millie replies.

"WITH THERE BEING a dead foot on the back porch, I was a little preoccupied, but I caught a glimpse of your garden this morning," Millie pipes up from the passenger seat as we head to Daphne's shop. "I've heard some of the other witches talking about getting clippings from your plants, but I had no idea it was so...*amazing* back there."

I grin and reach for her hand. I find myself

constantly reaching for her, needing to touch her. To reassure myself that she's here, and that she's whole.

"Thanks."

"You just planted it out of the goodness of your heart for other members of the coven?"

"Yes, and no. My property is quite big, and I'm not the type who enjoys mowing the grass all the time."

"You planted special herbs and flowers because you don't like to cut the grass? I might have been born at night, but it wasn't last night."

I laugh and make a right turn. "I don't want to freak you out."

"*Now* you don't want to freak me out?"

"Okay, point taken. You've planted a garden like that one many times over the past several hundred years. I know what you prefer to grow, where you like it, and I planted it myself because I hoped that the day would eventually come that I'd share my home with you again. And, if you want to get extra weird, I will admit that the house I live in now is the same one we lived in together. Before."

I risk a glance in her direction and see her staring ahead, likely processing what I've told her.

"Whoever owned the house after us tore out your garden, but when I bought it back, I replanted it."

"Why can't we be a normal couple?" she asks. "Just a normal, run-of-the-mill couple, who likes to have sex all the time and watch old eighties movies. Maybe pick up a hobby together, like bowling or skiing."

"There's no skiing in Louisiana," I remind her.

"You know what I mean."

"I don't know why. And, honestly, I wouldn't change it. Because I think you're amazing, and spending ten lifetimes with you is more than what most people get with those they love."

"You're quite sweet," she says. "In every memory I have, you're protective and affectionate and just *good* to me."

"There's enough shit in your life, darlin'. You don't need any more from me. And shouldn't one be kind to their beloved? Shouldn't I treat you as if you're a treasure? Because you are. I know that makes me sound ridiculously old fashioned, and maybe a bit too mushy, but it's true. I'm not one to be an asshole to the one who means the most to me. Especially when I never know how long we'll have together in a lifetime."

"It's not mushy." She kisses my hand. "And I was thinking just last night that I'm done wasting time, Lucien. What we have is too precious to waste. If you want me to move into your home, *our* home, with you, I will. Sanguine and I can move over today, and we can slowly shift the majority of my things over a little at a time."

"I'll hire movers," I suggest.

"We have a coven of people who'd love to help," she reminds me. "And I'll take them up on it. We'll make it work."

"Thank you." I park in front of Daphne's store, cut the engine, and turn to Millie. "I mean it."

"I know." We lean in and kiss, then nuzzle noses before getting out of the car and walking to the front door of Reflections, Daphne's antique store. Brielle unlocks the door and lets us in.

"Everyone's here," she says as we follow her to a little cluster of couches on the showroom floor where Cash is already seated. Brielle joins her husband, and Millie and I sit on a green velvet sofa across from them. Daphne paces the room, chewing on her thumbnail.

"You okay, Daph?" Millie asks.

"I'm agitated," she replies. "And, honestly, I'm freaked the hell out."

"Sit," Brielle says. "Let's talk this out."

Daphne sits in a pink armchair and smiles as she settles in. "A spinster woman owned this chair, and she enjoyed knitting and soap operas in her old age. She's quite the character."

"How can you own this place?" I ask her, intrigued. "Knowing that every single thing you bring in and touch will be a psychic event, and you'll never know if it's benign or sinister?"

"I have shields," she answers. "And a process to go through. Sometime, after all of this is over and we have free time on our hands again, you can come by, and I'll explain it to you."

"I'd be fascinated," I reply with a nod. "And I'll take you up on that."

"First," Cash says, getting right down to business, "let's talk about a dead serial killer who still has it out for these three women."

"Such a fun topic." Millie quirks a lip. "I think we can all finally agree that the man we saw dead on the street, and the severed body parts that have shown up, are his work. I don't know *how*, but it has to be him. He's also left blood smears for us to find. He's back to taunting us. Or, *me*, anyway."

"My dreams are changing," Daphne says. "I didn't want to mention it before until I knew for sure, and it's not the same as it was when Brielle was the focus. Then, I simply stepped into her dreams and watched as if it was a movie."

"What's it like this time?" I ask.

"Millie's always had the dreams." She looks at her sister. "Even when we were small, her dreams frightened her, and she'd come find one of us to sleep with."

I hold Millie's hand more tightly at the thought of her as a frightened child.

"I've never really been a dreamer, that's not my gift," Daphne continues. "Nor is it Brielle's. But, for some reason, I start to dream whenever *he* starts making an appearance. So now I'm going back in time, obviously to previous lives."

I lean forward, instantly captivated.

"I see Lucien and Millie, fighting together and losing every time. They're dressed differently and even speak different languages. They can't hear me or see me, and it's like I'm watching a rerun on TV. It's fucking frustrating."

"How is he doing this?" Brielle asks. "He's a *spirit*."

"It's not unheard of," I reply. "Poltergeists exist. Move things around. You hear all the time about people with haunted houses, and their things being moved. It's not out of the question, given how strong of an entity he is, that he can do these things."

"Stanger things have happened," Millie mumbles and then looks around the room as everyone stares at her.

"Really?" Cash says. "Stranger things than *this* have happened to you?"

"It's an expression." She waves him off. "I think the hardest part now is going to be finding him, given that he isn't in a physical body, and we have no idea where he's keeping his victims. And while we're on that subject, why is he suddenly killing men? It doesn't make sense. He has a thing for us, and he killed Brielle over and over again. He should be killing *me* over and over again if he stays on the same course. The men don't make sense."

"He's a fucking psychopath," Daphne reminds her. "And a sociopath in some regards. I don't think making sense is high on his priority list."

"Well, there's that," Millie says.

"Do you have the bloodstone with you?" Brielle asks Cash.

"Actually, I do." He takes a plastic bag out of his coat

pocket. "I brought it for you, Lucien, to add to the other two for examination."

"You're just walking around town with a bloody stone in your pocket?" Millie asks. "Murder cops are weird."

"So are witches." Cash winks.

"I want to touch it," Daphne says. "Maybe if I hold it, I'll be able to see where he is, determine how to find him."

"That's worth a try," I agree with a nod. But when Daphne reaches for the stone, she gets a shock that sends her back several feet.

"Ouch."

"That's what happened to me yesterday." Millie shrugs.

"Let me try." Brielle says, and the same thing happens to her. "Okay, so he's cast a spell on the stones and has blocked us that way."

"There has to be a way to find him. To lure him out," Daphne insists.

"Oh, yes, let's taunt him," Brielle quips, but I'm already nodding.

"She's right. The coven is having a special ritual on All Hallows' Eve, under the full blue hunter's moon. We may be able to cast the circle and force him out."

"Now, that's something worth researching," Millie says, reaching for her phone. "I'm going to call Miss Sophia and see if she can help with that."

Cash's phone rings in his pocket. "This is Cash." He

listens for a moment. "I'll be there in thirty. No one touches that scene, understood? Block it off and start getting statements."

He hangs up and runs his hand down his face.

"Dead body was just discovered in Audubon Park."

Millie flinches next to me.

"And?" Brielle asks.

"He's missing a hand and a foot."

CHAPTER TWELVE

"The dead won't bother you, it's the living you have to worry about."
—John Wayne Gacy

There's a war happening inside his head, and he's too exhausted, too spent from killing his last toy to fight as hard as he wants to.

He wanted to make it last longer. He'd cut off and cauterized the wrist, did the same with the foot, but the pain was too much, and the toy died.

It made him furious. It's like the toy didn't even *try* to work through the pain. To do as he suggested and just breathe, to go to a nice place in the mind.

No, the fucker just gave up.

And that was a huge disappointment. It seems he's

been dealing with that constantly, one big disappointment after another.

But this one drained his energy. He had to drag the body through the house and into his car, and then through the park to just the right spot.

That would have been taxing on him when he was still alive.

Plus, he's beginning to think maybe he made a mistake in the human he decided to use as a tool to complete his work.

Because they're fighting him. Trying to take back the body he rightfully stole.

His hand shakes as he reaches for his phone, not of his own volition, and types a note:

GET LUCIEN

The phone falls to the floor, and he collapses next to it, a grin on his face. Oh, yes, he'll get Lucien.

Don't you worry.

He just needs some sleep. Some rest to restore the energy and make him strong again, and then he can get back to work. With giving each toy the attention they deserve, making sure that Millie doesn't forget he's always nearby, and setting his next moves into motion, he's been busy.

He is a hard worker, after all.

But even those with the best work ethic need to rest, so he'll just take a nap to recharge his spirit.

The next phase of his plan is almost ready, and it will require all of his resources.

CHAPTER THIRTEEN

Millie

The wisteria is blooming. The arbor Lucien built for me behind the house, where we've set chairs and a little glass table for eating during every season except summer, is full of the heavy, purple blooms. It smells sweet and lovely, and is a welcome sight.

Purchasing this home in the Garden District of New Orleans was a dream come true for my husband and me. He worked long hours at the hospital to earn enough money to afford it, and I don't take one day for granted in our grand, white house with its green iron railings that keep the evil spirits at bay.

Well, that's the legend anyway.

They don't really keep anything at bay, especially things of the spiritual variety.

But it's a lovely thought.

I look in on our sweet Sabrina, only nine months old and napping in her carriage. My familiar, Tarot, lurks in the garden, chasing butterflies before taking a leisurely nap in the shade.

With both of my sweet ones safe and nearby, I get to work harvesting some lavender, rosemary, and a little mugwort. I look in on the tomatoes and carrots and pluck a few cucumbers for a nice salad later.

I've just finished filling my basket when the darkness descends, leaving me completely blind.

"You can't fool me," I say aloud, my voice perfectly calm despite the quick pulse in my neck. The taunts have come more often of late, just as Lucien said they would.

Lucien's just inside, and I try to talk to him through our special door. We cast the spell three years ago and never closed it.

I need you in the garden.

I feel the words slam against the side of my mind as if they're stuck there. How did he close our door?

"Lucien!" I yell but am met with only an evil laugh.

"Millicent, you know the only man that can protect you is me. Not that pitiful excuse you married. Only me. When are you going to learn? When will you see?"

I start to chant, the words Lucien made me promise to memorize for moments just like this one.

He's not laughing now.

"You dumb bitch! You can't escape me. You can't escape your destiny. I'll show you."

The blackness clears, and I'm once again in the garden with Tarot, weaving between my legs and meowing, and Sabrina sleeping soundly in her carriage.

What in the hell is happening?

I hear Lucien's voice now, and I know he's running through the house to the back door. I turn just as he slams out of the house and runs down the steps to me.

"He was here," *I say, immediately relieved when he wraps me in his strong arms.* "He tried to confuse me again. I used the spell you gave me, and he left. Angry."

"I'm sure he did." *Lucien's voice is hard.* "He grows stronger, Mill. We need the others. The six."

"I know," *I reply, feeling helpless.* "But I can't make my sisters understand or even want to help us."

"He's managed to block their gifts in this life," *my dear one says in frustration.* "It could lead to our defeat."

"Don't say that."

I sit up, gasping for breath, and find that I'm safe and in bed at Lucien's house.

Our house.

The house from my dream.

It's a beautiful historic home in the Garden District of New Orleans that wasn't even new when we bought it in the last lifetime. It's *old*. If I remember correctly, it was built in about 1850, predating the civil war. But it's been lovingly cared for and updated. A person would never know that it's almost two hundred years old.

I feel Lucien shift next to me, and suddenly, a single candle springs to life at the side of the bed, casting us in a soft glow.

"Are you okay?" he asks.

"Yeah, I just had a dream. Or a memory, I guess." I

fill him in and turn onto my stomach, bracing my head on my hands as I watch his handsome face, his eyes still filled with a little sleep. "I loved this house then."

"Yes, you did."

"You made me feel like a queen when you bought it for me."

He smiles and drags his finger down my cheek. "Good. I hope you still love it. If you don't, we can move."

"I mean, the real estate must be worth a fortune now," I say as if I would *ever* consider selling this house. "Much more than the twenty-six thousand dollars you paid for it once upon a time."

He shifts closer. "You *are* remembering more."

"Yeah, it's coming in little bits here and there. I don't want to leave this house, Lucien. It's beautiful. Big, but gorgeous."

"Well, just let me know if you get tired of it."

"Aren't *you* attached to it? I mean, you bought it back."

"It's only sentimental to me because *you* loved it so much. I don't need a house this big just for me."

I lean in and kiss him, then slide my body over his in one fluid motion, needing the connection that only comes from making love with him. I let the dream slide away until it's only this.

Only us.

"So, are you guys, like, gonna get married?" Daphne asks me a few days later. Witches Brew closes soon for the day, and I'm sitting in the reading area with my sisters, enjoying some needed time with them while Esme closes up the dining room.

I owe Esme a raise. She's been kicking ass this week.

"He hasn't asked me," I admit with a shrug.

"If he does ask?" Brielle inquires.

"Sure, I'll marry him. Again."

"It's so weird," Daphne says, shaking her head. "If we've all lived throughout all these different lifetimes over the past thousand years, why don't Brielle and I remember, too?"

"Because that's not how it's meant to be for us," Brielle answers. "Because this part of the journey is for Millie and Lucien."

"Which means I'm next." Daphne sighs.

"We've been told since this began that there will be six of us," I remind her. "Cash and Brielle, Lucien and me, and you and someone."

"I don't know who," she says, exasperation almost pouring out of her.

"You're being stubborn," Brielle adds. "Of course, you know *who*. You're just being difficult."

"I hate to burst your fairy tale bubble, but Jackson and I aren't together."

"That doesn't mean he isn't for you," I say, my voice gentle. I know how bad it hurt when Jackson walked out of Daphne's life, and how she's longed for him ever since. "It just means it was bad timing. You were hardly more than children when you met, Daph."

"I don't want to talk about him."

We hear footsteps coming from the dining area, and we all immediately stop talking, not wanting anyone to be privy to the conversation.

And then, I'm quite sure my eyes just about bulge out of my skull when Jackson himself walks into the room.

"Hello, ladies."

"Hey there," I say, glancing at my sister, whose face has gone paper-white. "This is a surprise."

"I wanted to stop in to see how you're doing and ask if it would be possible for you to get a message to Daphne for me, but...here she is."

"Here I am," Daphne says coldly. "I don't want your message, Jack."

"I need to talk to you."

"I changed my number for a reason."

"Yeah, because you're stubborn, and you won't let me *talk*."

Daphne studies her fingernails, avoiding looking directly at the handsome man. He's tall and muscular, and to top it off, a military hero.

I couldn't make this up if I tried.

And right now, he's gazing at my baby sister as if she hung the moon—blue or otherwise.

"Fine. I see nothing's changed here. But I didn't do anything wrong, Daphne." He leans in and whispers something in her ear that has her lip quivering, then he nods at Brielle and me and walks right out.

"What did he say?" I ask, though I already know. I'm not ashamed to say I dropped my shield long enough to eavesdrop.

She's my baby sister.

"It doesn't matter," she whispers.

"Daphne, you're only torturing yourself *and* him."

Daphne brushes her red hair over her shoulder and then wipes a tear from the corner of her eye.

"I can't give him what he wants."

"And what is that?" Brielle asks.

"Forgiveness," I reply for her and reach over to wrap Daphne in a hug.

"No, that's not it," Daphne says, shaking her head. "I forgave him long ago."

"Then what is it?" I ask.

"Truth. I can't give him the truth he seeks. And that means we don't have trust. We can't be together, you guys. Which means, Jack isn't one of the six."

Oh, baby sister, you're so wrong.

⸻

"I should go with you."

I lean against the kitchen counter and stare at Lucien. The man is giving me a headache.

"I'm a grown woman. I don't need a babysitter. Yes, I'm going to a mental hospital, but—"

"I'm not patronizing you, there's a madman out there who very much enjoys torturing you psychologically, and we don't know what he's planning next. A mental hospital is a breeding ground for vulnerable psyches, which means he could hurt you there. I'd rather be nearby."

I slip my hand into his and squeeze it three times, immediately softening at his concern. I know he's not trying to control me, he's trying to look after me. "If it makes you feel better, you can drive me. But I really want to go in by myself to see Mama. I have questions, and if you're there, I'll just be distracted."

"Why is that?"

"Because you're hot. Don't act like you don't know."

He laughs and brushes his thumb across my forehead, taking away any trace of my headache.

"I'm just an average guy, darlin', but it's good for my ego that you think I'm more than that. I can do some work from the car while you're in with your mom."

"You have a microscope in your car?"

"No, smartass, I have a phone, and I can answer emails and make some calls."

I nod and gather my bag and keys, along with the gift I got to bring with me, and we walk out to the car. Thanks to traffic, the drive over to the hospital takes longer than usual, but we make it all the same.

"I won't be long," I assure him and lean across the console to kiss his lips. "Less than an hour."

"I'll be fine," he assures me.

I walk inside, check in with security, and pass through the metal detector, then make my way up to Mama's floor. I'm nervous. I haven't been here to see her alone since she came to live here last year. Usually, I have one or both of my sisters with me.

But I've been thinking about what Miss Sophia said. I need to talk with Mama, to explain some things and ask some questions so we can both heal. I can't continue harboring animosity toward her. That will only fuel the hate and anger from *him*, and in the end, help him win.

That's not an option this time.

I find Mama sitting in a chair by the window, looking outside. I walk over, making a wide berth so she's sure to see me in her peripheral vision, and smile when she looks up at me.

"Hi, Mama."

"Millie." She smiles and glances around. "Are the other girls here, too?"

"No, it's just me today," I say and sit in the chair next to hers. We're facing each other at a ninety-degree angle. "I brought you a present."

"Oh, how sweet," she says. "This is a wonderful surprise."

"Go ahead and open it," I urge.

She parts the tissue paper in the gift bag and pulls out the small box inside. "My favorite chocolates."

"I remember you loving those when I was little," I say. "I thought you might like them."

"I don't even know when the last time was that I had these." She lovingly runs her hand over the top of the box. "Thank you, sweetheart."

"You're welcome." I clear my throat. "I also wanted to come in and talk with you, Mama. You see, I've been angry since you told us that you're a witch."

"I know, I could see it in you," she says. "I just don't know how to change it."

"I don't either, but I think talking about it might help."

"Honey, I'm always happy to talk to you. I'll tell you anything I know, and if I don't know, I'll do my best to find out."

My lip quivers, and I press them together as I try to collect myself.

"Why does that make you emotional?" she asks.

"Because this person sitting across from me is the mother I longed for all of my life. Mama, I'm a hedgewitch."

"Oh, that's wonderful."

"And now that I know I could have been learning from you all this time, I guess I'm grieving for everything we lost. And my first reaction was to be angry."

"You ain't got nothin' to be mad about." The words snap out of her mouth in a thick Cajun accent, and then Mama's eyes go round, and she clears her throat. Her eyes are changing from brown to blue. "I'm sorry, honey. Of course, you're angry. I'm mad, too. I lost all that time with you girls, and the way you were treated is just horrible. I'd give anything to be able to go back and change it all."

"I know you would." My words are careful now as I watch the physical transformation happening in front of me. She's starting to hunch a bit and suddenly has a twitch in her left cheek as she looks around, as if she's confused about where she is.

"Mama?"

"Huh?" She eyes me and then scowls. "Who are you? I ain't got no chillins."

My hand immediately flies to the amethyst around my neck, and I start to chant the spell from my dream, the one Lucien made me memorize a lifetime ago. I watch as whatever or whoever has taken over my mother's body turns from confusion to rage.

"You stop that," she growls. "You won't bring that voodoo hoodoo shit around me. You stop it right now."

She stands and raises her hand as if she's going to hit me, but I duck out of the way and keep chanting, starting over at the beginning when I reach the end.

Lord and Lady, lend me your might.
Guardians of the Watchtowers, make this right.
Ancestors and guides, hear my plea.
Toxic energy there will no longer be.
Evil and darkness be out of my life.
Leave my space with only light.

But it doesn't help. She only gets angrier as she curls her lip. With wild eyes, she forms her fingers into claws and comes after me. The noises coming out of her mouth don't sound human as she's suddenly pulled back from behind, two men in scrubs holding her arms.

A nurse comes running with a syringe and plunges the needle into Mama's arm, only infuriating her more.

"What's going on?"

Lucien's suddenly at my side, and his eyes take in my mother from head to toe.

"Ruth." His voice is loud and strong. "Ruth, I know you're in there. You fight back, darlin'. Whoever's got you has no right to you."

Mama's slumping now from the medication, and all signs of the being that possessed her is gone. She's crying softly, murmuring, "*I'm so sorry,*" over and over again.

"Mama." I frame her face in my hands. Her brown eyes, now free of the blue, look back at me. "It's okay, Mama. I love you. We're going to protect you."

"You can't," she whispers before she falls asleep and is carried away on a gurney to her room.

Lucien and I wait for her doctor to examine her, and then we meet with him in his office.

"It's not abnormal for patients to have moments of regression during their treatment," he says.

"That's not what this was."

His eyebrows shoot up to his hairline as he stares at me from across the wide, expensive desk. "And where did you get your psychology degree?"

He's not going to listen to me.

"You're right," I reply. "It must be *regression.*"

"We've given her a sedative. She should be back to herself tomorrow."

"I'll check in on her." I stand and nod at the doctor, then lead Lucien out of the hospital. Once we're in the car, I let the pent-up words out. "That motherfucker. Misogynistic asshole thinks he has all the answers, and I should just smile and nod. What a prick. What a piece of shit."

"But how do you really feel?" Lucien asks as he pulls out of the parking space and drives away from the hospital.

"She didn't regress."

"Tell me everything that happened from the minute you stepped inside that place," he urges. His voice is still hard, angry. He rubs his hand over his lips, moving back and forth in agitation.

The man I love is good and pissed off.

I relay the information, word for word. "And then you were there. How did you know I needed you?"

"The spell you were chanting," he says. "Not only is it for fighting *him* off, but because I created it for you, infused it with my energy when I recorded it with the Akashic Records, it automatically links you to me, as well. I'll always know to get to you as quickly as possible."

"Well, why didn't you say so?"

"I didn't know you still knew it."

"It was in my dream the other night." I swallow and lean back in my seat. "Lucien, taking Mama to the house was the wrong thing to do. The damn spirit or demon or *shadow* or...whatever it is, reattached itself to her."

"Something definitely happened," he agrees. "We need to go back tomorrow, armed with your sisters, some potions, and a stronger protection spell."

"We have some work to do."

CHAPTER FOURTEEN

Millie

It never ceases to amaze me how many people we can pack into Miss Sophia's house. Her cottage isn't big, but whether it's just her and I here, or thirty members of the coven, everyone fits as if she cast a spell to expand and contract her home as needed.

And knowing the older witch as well as I do, it wouldn't surprise me if she did exactly that.

My sisters are here, of course, along with Lucien's parents, Mallory Boudreaux, and Miss Sophia's granddaughter, Lena. Esme said that she wouldn't miss it for the world, and she's got her head buried in a spellbook, doing research.

Cash sits at the dining room table, directly across from me. Everyone here is researching the mystical arts, and my sister's husband is doing what he does best: searching for a killer.

As a former profiler for the FBI, and currently

working as an investigator with the New Orleans PD, Cash has vast experience hunting killers. He helped us find this madman once.

I know he'll do it again.

Lucien passes me a book and takes the one I have in front of me.

"Let's trade, darlin'," he says. "You're just staring blankly at this one."

"Why do I feel so lost?" I ask and shake my head. "Like I don't know where to start? We have two things happening. An undead psychopath is after us, and our poor mother can't shake the goddamn spirit that's intent on inhabiting her body."

"That's why you can't focus," Lucien replies. "You're overwhelmed, and rightfully so. Just breathe. Drink Miss Sophia's tea and center yourself. You have a room full of witches here to help you."

"I'm not a practicing witch," Brielle reminds us. "And neither is Daphne. How can we possibly help?"

"Whether you use your gifts for the craft or not," Miss Sophia replies from across the room, where she's stirring something in her cauldron, "you have the Power all the same, child. Joining the coven is always your choice. You'd be welcome here for that, as you are always. But if it's not for you, that's perfectly fine, as well. We're going to teach you the spells to chant with Millicent and Lucien tomorrow because the two of them can't do this alone. Cash, you'll join them, as well."

"Me?" Cash asks, looking around at us. "I have *zero*

gifts. I hate to disappoint you here, but I can't even make a good cup of coffee."

"You're one of the six," Miss Sophia reminds him calmly, not even looking away from her cauldron. "That's all the Power you need."

Mallory walks by, and I catch her attention. "Hey, Mal, I keep meaning to call Charly to ask if she wants a booth at the Halloween street fair again this year, and I keep forgetting. Do you know if she wants one?"

"Yes, she definitely wants one. She has some fun things planned for it."

"Great, I'll make sure she has space. And I'll do some shopping while I'm at it. I need some new work shoes."

"You should splurge on non-work shoes, too," Mallory says with a wink and keeps walking to where Lena's waiting with some essential oils for their part of the spell we're building for tomorrow.

Lucien's mother, Gwyneth, is in the kitchen with her husband, Aiden. She looks up at me, pats her husband on the shoulder, and then makes her way over to sit next to me at the table.

"Hello, dear." She places a slice of cake in front of me. "You should eat something."

I've known Lucien's parents for as long as I've known Lucien. They're part of the coven as well, and they've always been kind to me.

I can't help but wonder how much they know?

"Thank you," I reply and take a bite of the cake. I

know there must be some sort of potion mixed in here. A witch doesn't serve food that isn't laced with something helpful.

"This will help calm your mind, but not make you sleepy," Gwyneth says. "How are things at your lovely café?"

"They're great, but I feel bad for Esme. She's there all the time and covering for me more and more with all of this going on. I really need to hire a couple more people."

"I can't tell you how happy I am to hear that." Gwyneth smiles. "Because I'd like to apply for a job."

I stare at the other woman in surprise. "You want a job at the Witches Brew?"

"Absolutely."

I look at Lucien, then back at Gwyneth. "You don't have to do that."

"I'm not doing it for you. Well, not entirely. Let's just say retirement isn't all it's cracked up to be, and I'm bored out of my mind most days. Aiden goes to work at his jewelry shop, and I'm home. I can only knit so many scarves, Millie. Save me from myself."

"You don't want to work with Aiden?"

"Our marriage works so well because we *don't* work together," she says. "I have references, a clean criminal record, and I know just the right amount of potion to add to anything."

"Well, I'd *love* to have you work for me. If you're sure."

Gwyneth claps her hands and then leans over to kiss my cheek. "Thank you. I'm going to go brag to Aiden that I just landed a job. And check in on the potion I'm making for your mother."

She hurries back to the kitchen, and I turn to find Lucien grinning at me.

"What?" I ask.

"They love you," he says with a shrug. "Always have."

"Do they remember?"

He looks over my shoulder to where his parents are. "No. But they know I do. And they understand what's happening now. They're powerful witches in their own right."

"I know," I say. "I've always enjoyed watching them work together during rituals. The magic between them is strong."

He wraps an arm around my shoulders and leans in to whisper in my ear.

"There is no magic more powerful than that between two souls linked by unconditional love, *a stór mo chroí*. They've been linked as long as we have, for just as many lifetimes. I can't wait to explore the magic you and I can make together."

He kisses my ear, leaving me breathless and covered in goosebumps.

"Okay, you two can get a room," Daphne says, just as Cash holds up his hand.

"I think I have something," Cash calls, getting our attention. "I've been compiling a list of missing persons with similar descriptions of the two men who have been found so far. I found twelve that have been reported missing in the past few months, all last seen in the French Quarter."

He picks up a remote and flips on Miss Sophia's TV, which he's tethered to his computer, then clicks some keys.

"Here are all of the photos, side by side. Tell me what they have in common."

"You don't know?" Esme asks.

"Of course, *I* know," Cash says. "I want to know if you guys see it, too."

We all stare at the images, and I stand to walk in front of the television, my arms crossed as I stare at the face of each man.

"They all have brown hair," I say. "But different facial features. They don't all have the same eye color."

"But they're all wearing glasses," Brielle adds from beside me. "Brown hair and glasses."

Everything in me runs cold as I turn to Lucien.

"It's you. He's not killing *me* this time around, he's killing *you*, Lucien."

The air swirls in the room as my anger soars.

"Millie," Brielle says, but I shake my head.

"That bastard is killing the man I love because he's trying to hurt me. He's trying to piss me off, which is working."

"He's teaching you a lesson," Lucien says. His voice is calm, but his eyes reflect my frustration. "He knows the best way to scare you, to hurt you, is to hurt *me*. It's been that way for centuries."

"Well, he's done his job. I'm pissed. And I'm not scared. I'm going to fucking *destroy* him."

"Millicent." Lucien's before me now and sets his hands on my shoulders. "Your anger fuels his power."

"Am I supposed to feel *good* about this?"

"Of course, not. Use it constructively. Yes, we're going to defeat him, but not like this. Bring the wind down. You're making a mess, darlin'."

I glance around the room to see papers flying and everyone's hair blowing.

Miss Sophia smiles.

I take a deep breath and will the wind away.

I didn't even realize I'd kicked it up so violently.

I don't know if I've ever been this angry before.

"He's fucking with what I love."

Lucien's blue eyes soften as he brushes his thumb over my forehead, calming me. "I feel the same way, *a stór mo chroí.*"

I nod and look around us again. Everyone's smiling. No one cares that their hair is a mess, and the room is messy. And for the first time, I see that all of Miss Sophia's candles are lit, and the hearth fire is much higher than it was a moment ago.

"I've been waiting for this day," Miss Sophia says as she joins us and takes each of our hands. "I'm so happy you've reconnected. I hate that it took this evil to do it, but having your souls entwined will work in your favor in ways you can't even imagine. I've rarely seen wind like that blow through and not extinguish the fire. Your combined magic is strong and will only grow more, day by day. Keep honing it. Practice. Love each other."

"That's not difficult," Lucien replies, his eyes never leaving mine.

"And when you're ready, we'll have your handfasting ceremony."

I don't have to ask what she means, and neither does Lucien.

"I don't want it to be when we're in the middle of fighting this evil," Lucien says.

"That might be the *best* time, child," Miss Sophia replies. "The love and strength between you is powerful. But I'll leave that up to you. I'm so happy for you. Blessed be."

"Blessed be," everyone says in agreement.

"I do *not* mean to be a killjoy," Cash says, "but now that we know he's targeting men with Lucien's general description, I need to know how to proceed. How is he luring them?"

"Could he have inhabited a woman's body?" Daphne asks. "Like, maybe he's picking them up in bars the way he did with the women before."

"Of course, it's possible," Lucien says.

"But unlikely," Cash adds. "The woman's body wouldn't be strong enough to do the damage that's being done. And you know I don't say that to sound sexist, it's simply biology. He's strung some of these men up. The cuts are deep. He's completely severed limbs, for chrissake. I don't think a female could do those things."

"I agree," I say, as I think it over. "I don't think it's a woman."

"Are the men gay?" Brielle asks. "Maybe he's luring them that way."

Cash shrugs and thinks it over. "They could be. We don't list sexual preference in a missing person's report. I can do some digging on that."

"The potion is about ready," Miss Sophia says. "Let's gather out back and begin the ritual for the spell."

This is one of the strongest circles I've ever been in. The gathering is full of energy and passion.

Once sacred space is made, Miss Sophia chants the words of Power, calling on the Watchtowers, deities, and spirit guides to protect Mama and banish the evil that plagues her.

"Lord and Lady, working for us and through us, Guardians of the Watchtowers and guides of all, lend us your might. We dedicate this potion to shelter and protect our sister Ruth." She tosses more herbs into the cauldron and raises her hands into the air once more.

"Bring her back to the light and banish this evil. As we gather here in perfect love and perfect trust, our shield becomes hers. Our strength, her strength. Raising the Power of three times three, this is our will, so mote it be."

When we're finished, the potion is bottled up, and we're on our way for the night.

Tomorrow will be a busy day.

"WHY'S IT SO *SLOW*?" Esme asks the following day.

"Because it's Tuesday in the offseason," I remind her. "But that's okay because Gwyneth is coming in for a couple of hours this afternoon for training."

"I love Gwyneth," Esme says with a grin. "She's so sweet and has a wonderful energy about her."

"I agree. She'll be great for the shop. Do you mind training her today while I go to the hospital with the others?"

"Do you really think I would say no to that when I know you're about to go rescue your mother from demonic possession?"

I grin at my friend. "Well, when you put it that way, I guess not."

The bell over the door rings, and in walks Lucien with his mother.

"Look who I found loitering outside," he says.

"I was enjoying the sunshine and admiring your fun sign." Gwyneth smiles. "The broomstick standing out of the coffee mug is so darn cute."

"Thanks. And welcome. You're going to work with Esme this afternoon, and I'll be with you tomorrow morning, if that sounds good to you."

"Honey, I'm just so happy to be here, it all sounds good to me. You go take care of your mama. Esme and I will be just fine right here."

"Thank you." Lucien takes my hand and kisses my knuckles. "I'll see you both tomorrow."

We walk outside, but rather than leading me to his car, Lucien points across the street.

"Do you mind if we check in on Dahlia? I texted her the other day and haven't heard back."

"Of course."

We cross the street, and before we can open the door, Dahlia opens it herself and then jumps when she sees us. "Oh, hi, guys. You startled me."

"Are you closing for the day?" I ask.

"Yeah, traffic's slow, I'm caught up on orders, and I thought I'd take the rest of the day to run a couple of errands. My damn phone fell and busted. I have to replace it."

"I was going to ask why I haven't heard back from you," Lucien says.

"That would be why. I'm a klutz. Sorry about that. But I should have a shiny new one later today. Did you need something specific?"

"I called to invite you out to Miss Sophia's place with us yesterday. We thought it would be a good learning experience for you."

"Well, damn it. Next time for sure."

"We won't keep you then," I say. "Have a good day, Dahlia."

"You guys, too!"

"I CAN'T LET YOU IN," the security guard says. "The doctor has put a no-guest block on your mother's chart."

"I'd like to speak with the doctor," I reply. My sisters, Cash, and Lucien are with me. "He knew I was coming today to check on her."

"I'll see if I can reach someone." He picks up a phone. Less than five minutes later, the doctor is down at reception, a look of pure male stubbornness on his wrinkled face.

"I'm sorry, everyone. Miss Ruth is still very tired and not up for guests today."

"I am going to see my mother today," I reply. Cash pats my shoulder and steps forward, his badge out.

"Unless you want me to bring a whole slew of legal issues into your hospital, you're going to let us up to see our family member. In her room. Alone. We have a right to be with her."

The doctor's nose flares in frustration, but finally, he nods at the security guard and walks away without another word. We're cleared through the metal detector and led up to Mama's floor.

I've never been in her room. She's usually in the communal area when we come to visit. When we walk through the door of room 636, I have to take a moment to breathe so I don't throw up.

"What in the actual fuck?" I ask.

There's nothing in the room except for a bed. And Mama's currently shackled to it, her hands and feet buckled into restraints.

"Who the fuck'r you?"

The voice isn't Mama's. It's deep and hoarse, and the way she's thrashing on the bed isn't human. Her moans are guttural as if she's snarling at us.

"We need to get this potion in her," Brielle says and then swallows hard.

"Oh my goddess," is all Daphne can say.

"Focus," Lucien directs, his voice calm but firm. "Let's begin the spell. Follow Millie and me. When we're finished, I'll get the potion in her mouth."

We gather around the bed. Lucien opens the window at his back, and with our hands clasped and a quick circle cast, we begin the chant.

This only angers the beast more. It shrieks and jerks, almost violently enough to break the chains.

The wind swirls around us as we finish the spell, and Lucien takes the potion from his pocket and holds Mama's mouth open as he pours the liquid inside.

The shrieking stops for just a split second, and then roars to life once more, as if the entity is in pain. Mama's back arches off the bed, and a gray shadow pours from her open mouth. It flies through the room and then leaves out the open window.

Lucien slams the window shut, and the room settles. Mama's lying still on the bed now, her chest rising and falling with shallow breaths.

"Mama?" Brielle says, brushing the sweaty hair off our mother's face. "Mama, are you there?"

"So sorry," Mama whispers weakly. "Shouldn't listen."

"Who shouldn't you listen to, Mama?" Daphne asks.

"Shouldn't trust."

"Mama, it's okay now. It's gone. And we cast one hell of a strong protection spell. You're going to be so much better now. So much safer."

"Not safe anywhere," she murmurs and then falls to sleep.

"I'm going to get a nurse," Brielle says and hurries out of the room. When she returns, she has two nurses in tow.

"She was possessed," I inform them. "You don't have to believe me."

"Oh, honey, I believe you," the older of the two insists. "When you've seen the things we have in this place, you know that literally anything is possible."

"Thank you. We've cast out the spirit and put a protection spell around her. She should be able to recover now."

"Can she have her furniture back?" Daphne asks.

"Of course. We'll return everything as soon as she wakes up and we see that she's back to herself."

The younger of the nurses hasn't said a word. Her fingers shake as she takes Mama's temperature.

"Are you okay?" I ask her.

"I'm new," she replies. "Just out of school. Never seen anything like this before. Or most of the things around here."

"She's green," the other nurse says. "It gets worse. And sometimes, it's much better. Now, don't you worry, we're gonna take real good care of your mama. She's in good hands."

When we're on our way out, Brielle stops in the middle of the hallway. She's staring straight ahead, and her face goes white.

"What do you see?" Lucien asks her.

"There are always a lot of shadows here," she whispers. "But this one is...different."

"How?" I ask.

"I see him," Daphne says, her hand on the wall.

I take Lucien's hand and lower my shields. Standing there, at the end of the hallway, is our father.

"Damn it."

CHAPTER FIFTEEN

Lucien

"Why is he fucking with us again?" Millie asks as she paces around the parking lot. "We got rid of him *years* ago."

"Who?" Brielle asks, looking completely confused. "It wasn't a *him* at the end of the hallway."

The sisters stare at each other.

"I saw a him," Daphne says, "but I have a feeling it's not the same him entity Millie saw."

They're outstanding to watch when the three of them are together. They have no idea how powerful they are when united, and yet the vast differences in their gifts, and even in the way they look, is startling. From Millie's fair curls to Daphne's fire-red hair and Brielle's dark waves, they couldn't be more different.

But they're linked in every way that matters.

"Dad was there," Millie says.

"I didn't see that." Daphne shakes her head.

"Me either," Brielle adds. "I saw a dead woman, covered in blood and trying to speak to me. Exactly the way they did *before.*"

"What did you see?" I ask Daphne.

She swallows hard. "Jackson's father."

"Oh, honey." Millie wraps her arm around Daphne's shoulders. I don't know the whole story of what happened between Daphne and Jackson, but it must have had something to do with his dad if Horace used him to fuck with Daphne.

"He's doing this on purpose," I say, getting their attention. "Horace is trying to scare you, distract you. He's taunting you."

"Distract us," Millie murmurs. "From what he's doing? That doesn't make sense. The sick asshole has been *proud* of what he's doing."

"No," Cash says, speaking up for the first time. "He's distracting you from each other and from your inherent Power. If you're not concentrating on the task at hand, catching and destroying him, you can't do that. He wants your attention diverted, distracted, and he's using scare tactics to do it while simultaneously getting a thrill out of taunting you or *punishing* you. It's all a mind game for him."

"For fuck's sake," Daphne mutters and paces away in frustration. "How does he know what messes with us psychologically? How could he *possibly* know that seeing Jack's dad would make my blood run cold? It's not like I took an ad out in the paper and made it public knowledge."

"He knows pretty much everything about you three," I reply, thinking it over. "For most of your lives, he watched you from just outside the windows of your house. Then, he made it his business to follow you, to keep an eye on you every day. He's been stalking you for years."

"And why didn't we feel it?" Brielle asks. "Yes, we have shields, but we're psychic for the love of Moses. Why didn't we feel that he was near?"

"Smoke and mirrors," I reply. "Horace is excellent at smoke and mirrors."

"Stop saying his name," Millie murmurs, just as darkness descends on us. I can't see the others. I can't hear them.

I only hear maniacal laughter, as if *he's* having the time of his life.

Or his death.

I begin to chant the spell I taught Millie a lifetime ago. She's doing the same because I can suddenly hear her in my mind, feel her as if she's standing next to me.

Halfway into the spell, Horace snarls, the darkness disappears, and we're left standing in the parking lot as if nothing happened at all.

"I think we should all learn that spell," Daphne says.

"I'm happy to teach you," I reply with a smile.

MILLIE COLLAPSES on the couch in our living room with a huff and pets Sanguine, who walks circles on her witch's lap.

"Okay, I think we need to talk," Millie says.

"You're exhausted," I reply.

"Yeah. The psychic stuff drains me." She shrugs a shoulder. "I'm fine. I'd like to know how he defeated us in previous lives. In other words, what have we already tried that failed? I don't want to use that again."

"That's a good point," I say and sit across from her. "He wasn't always the cause of our deaths."

"Oh," she says in surprise. "I guess I just assumed he was. But now that I think about it, you were killed by witch hunters in Salem, not *him*."

"Exactly," I reply with a nod. "In some lifetimes, it was an illness or an accident. But I can write down the spells and weapons that didn't work before."

"That would help," she replies. "I'm going to keep reading my grandmother's grimoire. And Miss Sophia sent home a few other books for me to look at. I feel like that's all I do. Read. And use Google translate because I don't understand half of the languages, so that takes forever."

"You sound defeated."

"I'm not. I'm worried that I won't learn enough in time because he's escalating so quickly. I'm worried that I was too stubborn for too long and won't have much time with you."

"Stop that right now." I sit next to her on the couch

and pull her close. "We're going to defeat him this time. I don't know how I know, but I do. We still have resources to tap, and we're moving forward. This is nowhere close to being done, Millicent. Don't be discouraged. We'll get there."

She buries her face in my shoulder and takes a long, deep breath.

"Thanks. I needed that pep talk."

"Anytime."

"I could use a distraction from all of this," she says and looks up at me. "I haven't taken the time to really explore this big old house since I moved in. How about a tour?"

"Absolutely." I take her hand and pull her off the couch. "Obviously, the kitchen and living areas are down here, along with the laundry, what used to be a music room, a library—"

"A *library*?" she asks. "I didn't know about the library. Show me everything. Even the things I've already seen."

I kiss her forehead and then lead her from the living room to the music room.

"It's empty," she says.

"A lot of the house is," I reply. "But it can be filled however you like. This was a music room back in the day."

"This is the perfect spot for a baby grand piano." She goes to stand in the corner by the windows.

"Absolutely." Yes, that's where it was. And she played it beautifully. "Do you play?"

"No." She shakes her head. "No lessons are available to a kid when her single mother is possessed by an evil spirit."

"Good point." I lead her to the library. "The last owner left all of the books in here, and they said the owner before them did the same. I think some of these were here when *we* were here last time."

"Wow," she says as she lovingly brushes her fingertips over the spines of the books in the cases. The room is two stories tall with volumes from floor to ceiling and a ladder on rails for fetching things high up. "Maybe we stashed something in here that could help us."

"You know, you could be right," I reply, thinking it over. "I'll climb up later and do some digging."

"Maybe I can rotate some of the less valuable books through the café in the reading nook for customers to read."

"There's plenty here," I say. "That's a good plan."

She sighs and continues looking around, then nods. "Okay, what's next?"

"Upstairs is our room, and four other empty bedrooms, all with adjoining baths."

"Geez, Lucien, this house was ahead of its time when it was built."

"Not all of the bedrooms had adjoining baths when it was built," I reply as I lead her up the staircase. "Someone remodeled over the past thirty years or so and added them. It used to be six bedrooms and one bathroom upstairs."

"Ah, so it's been modernized."

"Drastically. And it needed to be. A house this old needs new wiring and plumbing. I think someone once planned to turn it into a B&B but ran out of money and had to sell."

"That makes sense," she says as we pass our bedroom and start opening doors to the other rooms. "I love the hardwood. Is it original?"

"The downstairs is, but all of the floors up here have been replaced."

She nods and looks into the bathroom, then a closet, before we move on to the next.

She stops before the closed door.

"What is it?" I ask.

"This was the nursery." She looks up at me for confirmation. I nod. "Her name was Sabrina. She was born in the spring, and she had Daphne's red hair."

"And her mother's brown eyes." I kiss the top of her head. "She was lovely."

She opens the door and steps into the empty room. White curtains hang on the windows, and someone painted the walls mint green.

"I have a really, *really* weird question."

"I'm ready."

"Lucien, do we have grandchildren out there? Great-grandchildren? Descendants?"

"That's not a weird question," I reply with a sigh. "And the answer is, I don't know. I haven't looked because what would be the point? I don't know what happened to Sabrina after we died. I don't know if she had children. But if she did, they could still be living."

"This is crazy," Millie says and leans against the wall. "And sad."

"Don't be sad." I kiss her lips gently. "Let's keep going, shall we?"

"Okay."

We look in on each bedroom and bathroom.

"That's it."

"There's a door right here," she says, already turning the knob.

"That's just the attic."

"Then it's a must-see." She flips on the light and leads me up the stairs to an open space that spans the entire house. "Whoa, it's huge. And pretty empty, just like the rest of the house."

"Lots of storage," I say and watch as she roams around the dusty space.

"Probably some spiders up here." She scrunches up her nose, then turns and examines the wall. "Wait a second. There's something about this area over here."

She wanders to the wall and stares at it.

"I don't think there's anything there."

"I swear, there's a hole, or a secret passageway or something."

"If there was anything, I'm sure a previous owner found it when they remodeled."

"It doesn't look like this area has been touched," she

says. "I'm telling you, I remember something about this space."

"Okay, let's figure it out. I don't remember there being anything out of the ordinary up here. You had some trunks stored up here full of old clothes, and some mementos. Baby things that Sabrina outgrew. Just the standard things that people put in attics."

"I wonder if..." She squats and starts running her hand along the wall. It's just clapboard, not sheetrock. Suddenly, a piece of the wall gives way, revealing a hole. "I *knew* it."

"Holy shit." I sit back, stunned.

"I made this hiding place," she says as she pulls her phone out of her pocket and turns on the flashlight, shining it into the darkness. "Ah, there it is. I can't believe I remember this."

"I can't believe what I'm seeing," I admit. "We never had secrets from each other."

Is that hurt I hear in my voice? Maybe. It's never been like Millie to keep something from me.

"This wasn't a secret from *you*," she says as she pulls a wooden box out of the hole.

"Is anything else in there?"

"No, just this." She turns off the flashlight and shoves her phone back into her pocket. She sits on the dusty floor beside me and blows dirt off the top of the box. There are two entwined hearts carved in the top. "I didn't remember this until we came up here. This is so cool. Like something out of a movie."

"Our whole lives are like something out of a movie, Millicent. I'm dying to know what's in that box."

"Okay, let's see if I remember how to open this thing. You push here, and tug there, and..." The puzzle box opens, and Millie smiles at me in excitement.

"What is it?"

She takes some dried flowers off the top. "These flowers were in my hair when we got married in the park."

The crown of blooms is faded from time but still intact. When the time comes, I'll revive them so she can use them again.

She gingerly sets the flowers aside, careful not to break any of them, then reaches in for the next thing.

"I wrote this letter," she says as her eyes fill with tears. The envelope is yellowed with age and sealed with wax.

"You should read it."

"Before I do, I need to clarify that when I stowed this all away, I didn't know that we'd ever be here again."

"Of course, not. We've lived all over the world, and each rebirth was random in time. Sometimes, it was only a few years later. Others, a hundred years passed before we were born again."

"Exactly. So, I didn't put these in the wall thinking that I'd find them again later. Everything in this box just meant the world to me, and I didn't want them to be someone else's."

"I understand, *a stór mo chroí*."

"Before I read the letter, look at this." She pulls out a tiny pair of shoes from the box and gives me a watery smile. "Her shoes."

"So tiny."

She sets the footwear beside her flowers, then opens the seal on the envelope.

"I'm nervous. I don't remember what this says." She unfolds the paper and clears her throat.

"Dear Lucien,

With your unexpected passing, I know that it won't be long before my life will also be finished. At least, this time around. I know I'll see you again soon, but the unknown of how long that might be leaves me with an unyielding ache in my chest. I long to hear your voice, to feel your strong arms around me, just once more.

Our daughter has gone to live with your parents. She's happy out on the farm with the animals and her very own puppy. They've promised me that they will teach her our ways and make sure she knows how very much we both love her.

I'm spending these last days in our house, committing every moment here to memory with the hopes that those memories will follow me through to the next lifetime, wherever that may be. Each life with you is precious, a mhuirnín, *but this one was extra-special. I was convinced that this would be the time we would grow old together, enjoy our children and grandchildren, and live a somewhat normal life.*

But that wasn't meant to be. I know you'd tell me not to be angry. That there's nothing we can do about the hand that fate dealt us.

But I am *angry, my darling. For you've been torn from me once again, and I'm left here to mourn you. My only solace is the knowledge that the pain won't last for long.*

You are my heart. My beloved. And my soul being linked to yours is the greatest joy and honor.

Because my time grows near, I don't want these few possessions to be found by anyone else. They're private, just between the two of us. I know I'll never be back here, in this time and place, but it's my hope that no one finds this hiding spot until the house is one day torn down. I've put a spell on this attic, ensuring that it will remain as it is for no less than one hundred years.

I love you, my treasure.

Millicent

Tears fall down her cheeks as she folds the letter and lovingly returns it to the envelope. Suddenly, she gasps, and her eyes find mine.

"Lucien, did I take my own life?"

"No." I pull her to me and kiss her cheek. "No, darlin'. Whenever one of us dies, the other does as well, not long after. A few months at most."

"I always thought dying of a broken heart was a cliché," she says. "But after reading this letter, I know it's not."

"No. It's not."

She hugs me tightly and then presses a kiss to my chest.

"Is there anything else in the box?" I ask.

"Actually, yes." She wipes her cheeks and reaches in

to retrieve another item. She comes back with a red pouch. She opens it and shakes the contents into her palm. "Oh my goddess."

Two gold bands wink in the light. They're strung on a piece of rope that's tied in a bow.

"Our wedding bands," she says.

"On the cord from our handfasting ceremony," I add softly, feeling close to tears myself. What a treasure this is! I would have thought that anything we owned before, aside from this house, was long gone.

"Lucien." She licks her lips as she tugs the bow free and untangles the rings, which look as shiny as the day I bought them in the French Quarter a century ago. My heart pounds in my chest, as I already know what she's thinking.

I don't need to be able to read her mind to know.

She's a part of me. We're two halves of a whole.

I know her as well as I know myself.

I take her hands in mine and look deeply into her beautiful brown eyes.

"Tell me."

"We don't need a feast and a priestess to bind our souls together. We can perform the ritual ourselves, whenever we want. It's our choice."

"I understand that. But I don't want to push you, Millie. I've been ready for a decade, but I'm happy to wait for you to be ready, too."

She shakes her head and makes a fist around our rings. "I'm ready."

CHAPTER SIXTEEN

"Have you ever tasted blood? It's warm and sticky and nice."
--Susan Atkins

"Oh, it's been a good day." He grins into the face of his toy. The man cries and says something unintelligible, but that doesn't upset him the way it usually would.

No, nothing can kill his good mood today. Everything is going so nicely now. Just the way he's wanted it to from the very beginning. His girls know he's nearby. They're getting the little gifts he's left for them.

Especially his headstrong Millicent. She's always been a willful child, but after this punishment is over, she'll understand that he's doing this for her own good.

Yes, he thinks to himself, *it will be wonderful*.

Now that his plan is in full swing and everything is as it should be, he's decided that now is the perfect time for him to play a little. To have an evening of enjoyment. He hasn't taken the time to practice and relax in far too long.

He can't let himself forget what he's already learned.

No, that won't do.

So, tonight is for fun.

"We're going to have the time of our lives tonight, Lucien." He claps his hands and turns to his toolbox, which he keeps on the opposite side of the room from the beds the toys lie on. "I think I'll use this beauty today."

He pulls out a hacksaw, a drill, and a cauterizer.

The toy keens in fear.

"Now, don't worry. I'm not going to take a hand or foot this time. We've already done that, and I don't like to repeat myself. No, I need to work on something a little more intense."

He crosses back to the toy, who promptly soils himself, peeing all over his naked body.

"Well, that's messy, isn't it?" He turns to the toy in the next bed. "You can clean that up later. Now, I have a new workbench! Did you see? It's beautiful, and going to be *so* much easier, really. You'll find this much more comfortable."

He jerks the toy from the bed over to the bench and manages to maneuver him onto his back.

"We have to retie your ankles and hands," he

explains. "I apologize. I hate to do that on my bench, but I'm not quite as strong in this body as I once was. But don't worry, it won't take away from the enjoyment of it all."

The toy isn't crying anymore. He's just lying still, staring at the ceiling, his eyes empty of emotion.

"Here we go, Lucien," he says and flips on the saw, then buries it in the toy's chest, right between the nipples.

Screams fill the air.

Blood runs like a river onto the floor.

Ah, yes, disemboweling always was his favorite thing. He works quickly but efficiently. And he rejoices when the life doesn't leave his toy's eyes until after the last piece of innard is removed from the body.

"I haven't lost my touch," he says with delight.

CHAPTER SEVENTEEN

Millie

I've never been surer or more ready for anything. Lucien and I are linked, have been for centuries, and it's only right to cement our union here and now, in our home.

I've changed into a simple white dress with cap sleeves, and a brown belt cinched at the waist. My hair is down around my shoulders, my makeup is minimal. But I feel beautiful and ready to be bound to the man I love.

Lucien walks into the bedroom from the bathroom and stumbles to a halt. He's fastening a button on his shirt, but his fingers still as he takes me in.

"It never fails to leave me speechless."

"What?"

"Your beauty. Your heart just shines through you. You're radiant, Millicent. In this and every lifetime."

"You're charming," I reply and step to him so I can

finish buttoning his shirt. "I think we should do this outside near the garden."

"I like that idea," he says and kisses my nose before turning away to fetch something from the bathroom. He returns, holding my crown of flowers, but they've been restored to fresh blossoms as if they were just picked this morning. "I thought you'd like to wear this."

"Oh, they're so lovely." I smell one of the flowers before placing them on my head. "There. All ready."

We walk downstairs and out back to the beautiful gardens. It's just past sunset, so the sky is deep purple, with the waxing moon our only witness.

Later, once all of this is settled, we'll have a formal ceremony with a priestess and a feast for all of our loved ones.

But for now, this union, this promise is just between Lucien, me, and the deities.

With a snap of his fingers, the lanterns around the garden's edge ignite in soft flames.

Lucien takes my hand and pulls our rope out of his pocket. It's actually three cords in three different colors, woven together.

"We chose gold for wisdom, red for passion, and purple for spiritual strength," I murmur as I grip Lucien's wrist, and he mine. "You wanted to add blue for fidelity, and I laughed because no other would ever turn my head."

He smiles and then stares down at me with so much love, my heart bursts with it as he begins the ritual.

"As this knot is tied, so are our lives now bound. Woven into this cord, imbued into its very fibers, are all our hopes, our Power, and the promise of our present life together."

He loops the rope around our hands, and I help him tie the knot, then repeat the words back to him.

"As this knot is tied, so are our lives now bound. Woven into this cord, imbued into its very fibers, are all our hopes, our Power, and the promise of our present life together."

Wind swirls around us as we tip our foreheads together and offer up a prayer of thanks, and then Lucien kisses me, sealing our promise and our connection.

This moment is as beautiful and meaningful to me as any other that would include a hundred people. An owl hoots above as Lucien brushes a piece of my hair behind my ear, cups my face, and kisses me for all he's worth, as if every time before this he held something back, and it's finally being set free.

"Follow me, wife," he says with a smile and leads me into the house and up the stairs to our bedroom. He unties us long enough for us to undress, but then reties the knot once more. "We'll stay connected all night."

"In more ways than one."

That makes him laugh as he snaps his fingers and the candles glow around us. But laughter soon turns to soft sighs as he slowly and methodically stirs my blood into a frenzy of hot need.

He braces our tied hands above my head, and while murmuring sweet words of love and vows of forever, seals the sanctity of the covenant we've made to each other.

I feel the Power moving through me, the intense strength of our vows and our union. The room's energy intensifies with our Power, and then later, when we're sated and calm, the vibrations calm with us.

"I feel the shift in our Power," I say as I drag my fingertips lazily up and down his arm. "It's incredible."

"And will continue to grow. It's important that we do what Miss Sophia said and practice."

"We will." I snuggle against him, trying to get even closer. "But not tonight."

"No, *a stór mo chroí*, tonight is just for us."

───────

"THANK the goddess Café du Monde is open 24/7," I say as we climb the steps of our front porch.

"These are better eaten outside," he says and leads me to the porch swing.

We'd intended to keep the rope tied around our hands all night, but about an hour ago, I said I was craving beignets, so we pulled the cord through, making the knot, and got dressed to go get takeout.

It's 4:30 a.m., so we kept the rope tied for a good stretch of time.

And who can say no to fresh beignets?

Not this witch.

We're sitting side by side on the swing, listening to the cicadas as we munch on the still-hot treats, covered in so much powdered sugar, I'll look like a ghost when we're finished.

I don't care.

"The sign says they've been open since 1862," I say as I chew and then sip my frozen café au lait. "And if we were here after that year, I'm going to assume that I'm so addicted to these babies in this life because I gorged on them in the last one, as well."

He laughs and wipes his mouth with a napkin. "They were your favorite, absolutely. When you were pregnant, you asked me to go get them for you at least three times a week."

I glance his way in surprise. "Wow, that's a lot of sugar. I bet I gained a hundred pounds."

"No, you didn't. And if you had, who cares? You were pregnant and wanted a treat."

"Wow. Are you a robot? Because you're pretty wonderful."

"I'm old," he says with a shrug. "I'm an old man in a thirty-six-year-old's body, Millicent. I always acted older than my age when I was a kid, and was teased for it, although I didn't care. I've been through so many lifetimes that I learned how to be kind and patient."

"So, you got your asshole years out of you about eight-hundred years ago."

He laughs again and then nods. "Yeah, I guess so.

My wild bachelor days when I was young and stupid were a long, long time ago. And, I love you. No matter what you look like, or what you eat, I love *you*. I always have. So, eat your sweets. I don't care."

"If I could find a way to clone and sell you, I could be richer than that dude who owns Amazon. You're exactly the guy that every woman is looking for."

"Well, I'm also a little overprotective, I don't always pick up after myself, and I once got a B in biology."

"*No*." I clutch my chest as if I'm completely appalled. "Well, never mind then. No one wants someone who got a B in biology."

I lick my lips and stare down into the empty bag.

"All gone?" he asks.

"Yep. That's okay." I brush off my hands and scoot closer to Lucien. He reaches out and gently brushes some powdered sugar off my cheek.

"You always were messy when it came to these."

"I mean, it comes with the territory," I say. "Okay, let's talk about something less fun."

His face sobers. "Okay. Is everything all right, darlin'?"

"Well, it will be. If you let me redecorate the master bedroom. It's just so *boring* in there, Lucien. It screams: I'M A MAN AND I DON'T CARE ABOUT LINENS. Do you care if I freshen it up a bit?"

He's laughing now, his fingers pressed to his eyes. "I thought you were going to tell me something horrible, what with everything that's been going on lately."

"Maybe this *is* horrible. Maybe you love your plain comforter and mismatched furniture. Did you get that at yard sales, by the way? How does a man who drives such a sexy car have such horrible taste in home goods?"

"I'm hardly home," he says and wraps his arm around me to tug me tightly against him. "I don't care where I sleep, as long as it's warm and comfortable. I told you, this house is yours. Decorate it any way you like."

"I don't want you to think that I'm coming in here and just changing everything. That's not it at all."

"You need to make this your home, Millie."

"You know, I don't think women would care about the B in biology, after all."

I sigh and lean on my man as we swing on our porch, listening to the very early morning sounds of the French Quarter.

"WE ONLY SLEPT FOR AN HOUR," I say as I stretch in the bed, naked and sated.

"So, play hooky today," he says and kisses my cheek. "Stay here with me, all day."

"I can't." Regret hangs heavy in my voice. "I'm meeting your mother at the Brew this morning so I can keep training her, and I have to start getting ready for the Halloween street party next week. Which, I just realized, is only a few days away."

"Well, damn."

"But I'll meet you back here later this evening."

"It's a date."

I kiss his chin and then roll out of the warm bed. Despite the little sleep I got, I feel energized and ready to start the day.

Is this what being blissfully in love does to a person? Gives one energy they didn't know they had?

Maybe.

I won't complain because I'm going to need the extra oomph if I'm going to get through this day.

Lucien and I dress at the same time, and I raise a brow. "Where are you headed so early in the morning?"

"I might as well go into the lab and get started on my day, as well. I have an early meeting, and few things to do to get ready for it."

"I know I said the other day at Miss Sophia's that everything we're involved in right now is cutting into my work and being available for the café. It has to be cutting into yours, as well."

"A bit," he says with a nod. I prop my hand on my hip and raise a brow. "Okay, a lot. There's nothing to be done about that right now, though. I'm an independent contractor, so I'm able to say no to requests if I need to. Right now, my priority is the work Cash is giving me and our journey. The rest will still be there when it's all finished."

I hug him tightly and cast a small protection spell over him. I feel him kiss the top of my head.

"Thank you for that."

"You felt it?"

"Of course."

"I'd like to mix a potion to put in your coffee, as well, but it doesn't look like I have time."

"Millie, I'm fine."

"He's hunting men who look like *you*," I say, voicing my fears aloud. "If you think that doesn't scare me, you don't know me as well as you think you do."

"I know it does, and I'm telling you right now that I'm careful and safe. I promise. I've only just found you again, I'm not likely to do something stupid to lose you so quickly."

"See that you don't." I soften my words with a kiss and then hurry out of our room and down to the kitchen, where I fill Sanguine's bowl and take a moment to pet the feline. "Good morning, sweet girl. Have a good day today. I'll take you to the café with me soon. If you'd stay in the reading room, you could go every day, but you're stubborn."

She rubs her cheek against my chin before I stand and reach for my bag and keys and smile back at Lucien.

"I'll see you later, love."

Before I can walk through the door, he catches my hand in his and tugs me to him, then kisses me long and slow until my mind buzzes.

"Have a good day."

The drive to work is easy, as it's still well before six in the morning and not many people are out and about quite yet. I used to be jealous of those who got to sleep in, but I'm used to the early morning hours now and enjoy the alone time at the café before my first customers of the day start filtering in.

The alley behind my shop is blocked today for maintenance, so I score a parking spot just around the corner, lock my car, and toss my keys into my bag as I walk around the block toward the front entrance of my little café.

There's no one around, but I feel a shift in the air as I get closer, and squint when I see what looks like something blocking my entrance.

"What in the world?" I mumble and then stop in my tracks and stare.

A man.

A man is strung up, hanging from his hands in front of my door. He's naked, and his torso has been sliced—no, *hacked* is a better word—open. His organs and intestines have spilled out, trailing down his body to the sidewalk below, where just a tiny pool of blood puddles under his feet.

I'm screaming inside my head, but I can't make any sound come out.

I can't breathe.

My eyes travel up the corpse and land on his face, where two things catch my eye.

One, he's wearing glasses.

And a bloodstone has been embedded in his forehead like some sick third eye.

I swallow hard and reach for my phone, automatically dialing Cash's number.

"I have a dead body," I say into the phone around the lump in my throat. "At my shop."

"I'll be there in ten minutes. Don't disturb the scene, Millie."

"No worries there."

I hang up and immediately dial Lucien, but it goes straight to voicemail.

If I have to stand out here by myself with this body, I'll go insane. This isn't just a hand or a foot. Or even a body in the street, surrounded by a horde of onlookers.

This is a disemboweled man, hanging in front of *my* door. The message is loud and clear.

It's a gift for me.

I back away, one small step at a time as if any sudden movements might wake the poor dead man and startle him. My foot falls off the curb, and then arms encircle me. I let go of the scream that's been stuck in my throat.

CHAPTER EIGHTEEN

Millie

"It's just me, dear."

I'm staring at Gwyneth, relieved that it's her and not a homicidal madman.

"Cash is on his way," I whisper. "My goddess, Gwyneth."

"I'm casting a spell so bystanders can't see this," she murmurs and swirls the air a bit with her fingers. "This is too brutal for anyone to witness."

It doesn't take long for Cash to arrive, followed shortly by other cops, and an ambulance.

"Where is it?" Cash asks.

Gwyneth gestures with two fingers and points to my front door.

"How did you—? You know what, never mind." He shakes his head and walks over to the body, then shakes his head again and looks back at me. "I'm sorry, Mill."

"Yeah, you and me both."

"I'll get this out of here as soon as I can. But we have to work the scene first."

"Unfortunately, I know the drill."

Cash's men quickly block off the area and get to work, and I take Gwyneth's hand and lead her around the back, not caring in the least that the alley is blocked. We enter the Brew from the back door.

"Why are the lights on?" I wonder, just realizing that everything's on, the music, the lights. I can even smell coffee. "Who's in here?"

We hurry through to the front of the shop, and I find Esme staring out the windows. She turns when she hears us approach from behind.

"Whoa," she says and clutches her chest. "You scared the shit out of me."

"Likewise. What are you doing?"

"I came to work." She gestures as if I should already know that. "You know, because I *work* here. What's going on? Why is there a naked dude outside the door?"

I glance down at my phone and try to call Lucien, but it goes right to his voicemail again. "Call me as soon as you get this."

Damn it, where *is* he?"

"You're not supposed to be here until ten," I remind her.

"You've been a little busy, Millie. I came in to help."

"Did you come in through the front or the back?" Gwyneth asks her.

"The front. I hate going through the alley. Gives me

the creeps. Besides, it's blocked off today. What's going on out there?"

"Was there not a body hanging by the door when you got here?" I ask her.

"A body? Uh, no. Pretty sure I would have noticed that. I've been here for almost an hour because I wanted to mop the floor one more time this morning. Someone spilled a full mocha all over it yesterday, and I wanted to make sure I got all the stickiness up."

"How is it possible that you've been here for an hour and didn't see anyone hanging a dead body in front of the door?" I demand.

"I haven't been out here this whole time. I spent some time sweeping the courtyard out back, and I straightened up the reading room. I had to clean the bathroom. Jesus, Mill, I do work here, you know?"

"What I know is that you're here when you aren't supposed to be, and I walked up on a dead body hanging outside of my business."

"What exactly are you accusing me of?"

"Hold on," Gwyneth says, holding up her hands. "No one is accusing anyone of anything. Millie, you need a minute. This is a scary thing, and you need to take a breath."

"I can't reach Lucien." I feel tears threaten. I need to hear his voice, know that he's okay.

"Go try to call him again," she suggests, and I follow her advice because I'm about to accuse Esme, a woman

I trust implicitly, of being possessed by Horace and hanging a dead man in front of my café.

That sounds ridiculous even to my own ears.

Just as I'm walking through the door to my office, my phone rings. "Oh, goddess, you're okay."

"Of course, I'm okay. I'm at work. What's wrong?"

I clench my eyes closed, relieved to hear his voice. I tell him about what I found when I arrived at the shop.

"He looks just like you."

"He's not me, darlin'. Is Cash there?"

"Yes, he and his guys are taking care of it. I'm sure we'll have some questions to answer, and they'll want to talk to Esme, who was here when I got in. It's weird, Lucien. She's not supposed to be here, and she says she didn't see anything."

"Do you honestly think he possessed her?"

I scrunch up my face. "I don't think so. I mean, she's acting normal, and we put one hell of a protection spell on this place. There's no way he could come inside."

"That's your answer then."

"Yeah." I blow out a breath. "I could have gone my whole life without seeing that."

"I'm on my way over. I just have a couple of things to wrap up here."

"Stay there," I insist. "I'm going to work, too. We have to live our lives, Lucien. But I need for you to work that spell again, the one you cast when we went to the old house in the bayou. I need a line directly to you.

It made me crazy that I couldn't reach you this morning."

"We'll do it later today," he says. "And we'll keep it open for as long as you like."

"Okay." I want to be in his arms so I can have a good cry. "How can I go from the happiest night of my life last night to the scariest one this morning?"

"Ah, baby. I'm so sorry. Let me come over there, just for a little while."

I sniff and reach for a tissue. "You're always welcome here, but I'm okay. Let's get through today, and then we'll figure out what to do. I think I'm going to start bringing Sanguine with me to work. She adds a level of protection."

"Agreed. We'll cast a boundary spell that keeps her in the reading room."

I smirk. "She'll love that. I'll see you soon."

"See you soon, darlin'."

He hangs up, and I take a minute to pull myself together. I wipe my eyes and nose, brush my fingers through my hair, and then walk back out to where Gwyneth and Esme are already talking with the police.

The body is gone, thankfully.

"I need to ask a couple of questions," Cash says. "First, are you okay?"

"I'm better now that I've talked to Lucien. I saw the glasses on that man, and—" I can't finish the thought.

"I know. I had a bad minute myself. Tell me exactly what happened this morning."

I run through it all from the minute I parked my car until Cash arrived on the scene.

"That's all I know. Aren't there street cameras or something you can check?"

"Yes, and my team has already put in a request for the footage. But we did the same when it was just a hand on the bench, and the footage was jumbled, so we couldn't see who left it."

"Of course, it was." I laugh without humor and drag my hand down my face. "Because nothing can be easy with this."

"I'm going to take the bloodstone straight over to Lucien. But there's already a difference in this body compared to the others we've found."

"What?"

"It still had blood in it. He didn't drain the body. Not sure what that means. I have to think on it, but I thought I'd tell you. I shouldn't, because this is an ongoing investigation, but hell, nothing about this is normal."

"Thank you." I impulsively hug my brother-in-law. "Thank you so much."

"I haven't caught him yet."

"You will." I kiss his cheek. "Blessed be, brother."

His cheeks flush, and he squeezes my shoulder. "Call me for anything, any time."

"I will."

He and his men clear out, and I sit in a chair, just staring straight ahead.

"You know," Gwyneth says, "if you wanted to just close for the day and take some time to rest and heal, no one would blame you."

I swallow hard. "That's what I want to do, but it feels cowardly. It feels like if I run and hide, *he* wins. I don't want to give him the satisfaction."

"Hell no, we won't give him that," Esme insists. "We're working today."

I smile at my friend. "I'm so sorry about earlier."

She simply shrugs. "It's a weird day."

"It's been a weird *year*," I reply with a laugh and push my hand through my hair. Gwyneth catches sight of my finger.

"Oh, honey. Did you and Lucien perform a hand-fasting ritual?"

I nod and smile with excitement as I stare down at the plain gold band. "Just last night. It was the right time for us. But don't worry, we're planning to have a celebration, later, after all of this mess has calmed down."

"I couldn't be happier," Gwyneth says and pulls me to her for a hug. "I'm so happy for both of you."

"Thank you."

"This calls for a little treat." Esme starts whipping up a concoction behind the counter. "It's too early for alcohol, but a fruity breakfast drink is just the thing."

"I'll take it," I say with a smile. "I haven't even told my sisters yet. It was a spur-of-the-moment thing, and it happened so fast."

I want to tell them that these are the rings we wore a hundred years ago. That I remember so much more, but those details are just for Lucien and me.

"To my son and his beautiful bride," Gwyneth says, holding up her glass. "Here's to many years of wedded bliss."

"WHY AM I elbow-deep in the business end of a pumpkin?" Cash asks. We're all at Witches Brew, at different tables around the dining area, carving Jack-o-lanterns. "I should be out there in the mean streets of New Orleans trying to catch a killer."

"First of all," I reply as I dump pumpkin seeds into a bucket, "don't be a Debbie Downer. Halloween is our Christmas. And our New Year, come to think of it." I smile. "We have about thirty Jack-o-lanterns to make because while yes, there are killers to find, there are also a whole bunch of kids who want to celebrate Halloween."

"Wow, that was a great lecture," Cash says with a grin.

"You're welcome. Now, paste a smile on your face and carve one into that bad boy there."

I have a Halloween playlist on my phone playing through the speakers, and we're actually having *fun*. No thoughts of demonic spirits and a killer. No researching spells and weapons to use against the undead.

Just me and my family, enjoying each other.

I didn't realize how badly I needed this.

"So, Lucien and I got hitched," I announce and glance up to find everyone staring at me. I bust up laughing. "You should see your faces."

"Holy shit, you're wearing a wedding band," Brielle says. "You're not kidding."

"And you didn't invite *us*?" Daphne demands. "What the hell?"

"Very subtle, darlin'," Lucien teases from beside me as he continues digging guts out of a pumpkin.

"It was just him and I, and it's not legal yet— although we all know that the piece of paper is just a formality. We're as spiritually bonded as it gets."

Daphne crosses to me and takes my hand, then brushes her fingers over my band.

"Oh, my," she says, her eyes wide. "Holy shit, Mill."

"I know."

"What?" Brielle demands. "What is it?"

"You can tell them," I whisper to Daphne.

"She wore this ring in another lifetime." Daphne smiles. "She was just as happy then as she is now."

"This is the *same* ring?" Brielle asks.

I nod and explain to them how I found the box in the attic.

"I never find cool stuff like that," Brielle says. "I only find dead people."

"I'd rather have this," I say with a laugh. "And don't

worry, we'll do the bigger party thing later. I just didn't want to wait."

"I think it's lovely." Daphne kisses my cheek. "Happiness looks good on you, sister."

I've just been hugged by Brielle and Cash when there's a knock on the door.

I glance at Daphne, who's glaring at the glass, and then unlock the door and open it. "Hello, Jackson."

"Hi," he says. "I'm looking for Daphne."

"You found her." I gesture for him to come inside, and I lock the door behind him.

"Hey, Daph. I'm leaving town in the morning, and I wanted to see if I might talk you into having a conversation."

"You're not good at hearing *no*, are you?" she asks him. When he just stands firm, she sighs and rolls her eyes. "Fine. Let's go out back."

Jack follows her through the café like a lovesick puppy.

"I wonder what they're talking about," Brielle wonders.

"None of your business." Cash kisses her squarely on the lips.

Lucien leans over and kisses me on my temple.

"What was that for?"

"I have hardly touched you all day," he says. "Do I need another reason?"

"I suppose not."

"I wonder if they're having sex back there," Brielle questions.

"Ew. Not in my courtyard."

"That could be fun," Lucien says as if he's giving it some thought. It makes me laugh.

"I'm not having sex in the courtyard. There could be bugs, or people watching."

"Maybe we should give it a try," Cash adds, glancing in Brielle's direction, just as Jackson and Daphne return, both looking miserable and angry.

"So, that didn't go well," I say.

Suddenly, the room goes dark, as if a huge cloud has covered the sun. We look around the room in confusion as the wind picks up, and lightning flashes against the windows.

"What's going on?" Brielle asks.

Lucien reaches for my hand as thunder roars. He snaps his fingers, lighting the candles I have set around the space, giving us some light. They flicker under the force of the breeze but don't extinguish.

"Something doesn't like that we're all together," Cash says as he reaches for Brielle's hand.

Once more, lightning and thunder flash and crash, the concussion shaking the building.

Jackson instinctively wraps his arm around Daphne's shoulders.

The wind howls, and thunder booms again, then suddenly stops as if a switch were flipped.

We stare at each other, everyone breathing hard and looking confused.

"Well, that was new," Daphne says. I see she's leaning into Jack, his hand rubbing up and down her arm in a soothing gesture.

I wish they could figure their shit out. It's obvious they belong together.

"Does this mean our fun Halloween staging party is over?" I ask.

"No," Lucien replies. "He can throw all the temper tantrums he wants, but we're going to live our lives and enjoy each other. After we set a little protection spell before Jackson leaves."

I look over at the man my baby sister still loves. He doesn't seem to be shocked by what just happened in the least.

"I don't need the spell," he says.

"You'll get one all the same," I reply, my voice leaving no room for argument. "Your magic is stronger with ours rather than alone."

"My magic is lost to me," he replies.

"All the more reason for the spell, then."

CHAPTER NINETEEN

"They bothered me, so I decided to kill them."
--Della Sorenson

H e's quite pleased with tonight's search. It was time for a new toy. At first, no one in the bar interested him. Most were too fat or didn't wear glasses. But just when he was about to call it a night, the perfect specimen walked through the door.

Already a little drunk, this toy was having a good time with his friends. In town for a bachelor party, he'd said.

Slipping the belladonna into the toy's beer hadn't been a problem at all. And suggesting that they leave the bar together was met with lusty delight.

For both of them.

Of course, for different reasons, but it's always easier to take the toy when they're willing, especially now that Horace is in this new, weaker body. If the toy can walk under his own power, all the better.

This one is strong. More muscles than he usually looks for, but the right height, with brown hair, and even wearing the right glasses. Yes, he's absolutely perfect.

"We're going to have so much fun," he assures the toy as he unlocks the door of his new playhouse and leads him inside. "Just back here."

"You know, I'm not feeling so good."

Horace grins as he watches the toy press his hand to his head in confusion.

"Come on now, Lucien, you just need to rest." Horace leads the toy to his playroom and helps him lie down on the mattress he has on the floor, across from the other toys' beds.

This one is going to be special.

The toy passes out in just the knick of time, and Horace smiles gleefully.

Yes, everything is going just as planned. He's feeling more and more like himself, stronger every day—certainly, more confident.

Suddenly, pain sears through him, sending him to his knees. He holds his head and tries to cast a healing spell, but the pain is too incessant to concentrate on the words.

He rests his forehead against the floor, and suddenly,

images of *the six* race through his mind. Together. Holding hands.

They're together, is his only thought as the pain racks his body from head to toe.

It's too soon. It's too fucking soon.

Suddenly, the pain leaves as quickly as it came, and Horace is able to sit back on his haunches and take a deep breath.

The new toy moans.

As Horace turns his head to look at him, the toy swings his leg out and kicks Horace in the chest, sending him back on his ass.

Horace reaches for his workbench, and as the still-disoriented toy writhes on the floor, trying to get to his feet, Horace retrieves a knife, grabs the toy by the hair, and slices his throat, from ear to ear.

"Damn it," Horace growls. "This isn't how it was supposed to be, Lucien."

He hurries to grab a bucket and tucks it under the toy's neck, trying to catch every drop of blood.

"I had such fun things in store for you. And now you've ruined it."

They've all ruined it.

As the body bleeds out into the bucket, Horace stomps to the bathroom and stares at himself in the mirror.

"You're so fucking *weak*. Just a woman. I *knew* better than to take a fucking woman. You can't be trusted, just like the rest. And now, you're going to ruin everything because you're not strong enough."

His lip curls as he snarls at his own reflection.

"I took you because you were always strong. Always so sure and ready for a fight. And now look at you. Well, you won't get away with this. You'll need to be punished for your weakness, just like my girls need to be punished for theirs."

CHAPTER TWENTY

Lucien

I've just finished stripping the last molecule of blood off the bloodstone collected from the body Millie found in front of her shop, and the test result is in.

The blood is from the same person as the others.

All four stones are lined up on my table, side by side. They're roughly the same size. Green in color—jasper—with veins of red hematite running through the smooth surface.

Hence why they're called bloodstones.

I sent samples off from each one for DNA testing, but those results still aren't in. So, while I know the blood came from the same person, I won't be able to say *who* that person is until those results come back.

And even then, unless the owner of the DNA is in the system for some reason, we may not be able to figure it out.

It's fucking frustrating as Hades.

I strip off my latex gloves and toss them into the trash, then pace my lab. Why the bloodstones? These are new. I don't remember Horace using them in any previous lifetime.

What is the significance? I know that for Wiccans, a bloodstone can be used for protection, courage, and even as an aphrodisiac.

The thought of that son of a bitch leaving a stone as an aphrodisiac for *any* of the sisters makes me sick.

But the protection idea might not be far off.

Without thinking, I reach out and pick up one of the stones. It's cool beneath my fingers. Smooth. And suddenly, I feel sick to my stomach. Nausea rolls over me in waves so badly, I have to set the stone down and run for the trashcan, barely making it in time to heave my guts out.

When I'm able to catch my breath, I rinse out my mouth and eye the stones.

I choose another stone to pick up, and almost immediately feel the nausea return. I set the stone down, take a step back, suck in a deep breath, and instantly feel better.

What in the actual fuck?

I pull my phone out of my pocket and call the one person who might have answers.

"Hello, Lucien."

"Miss Sophia, I have some questions for you."

"And I'm happy to answer them, as always. I'm actually in the city today. Why don't I stop by your lab and we can talk in person?"

"That's even better." I'd love for Miss Sophia to see the stones for herself. "When should I expect you?"

"I'll be there shortly."

"Thank you." I hang up and leave the lab area for my office and quickly call Millie.

"Well, hello there, handsome."

She never fails to make me smile. "How are you today?"

"I'm just fine, thanks for asking. We're filling orders, and I'm getting ready to go out and prepare for tomorrow's Halloween street party. We have tables and tents to set up, along with lights to string and all kinds of other chores. I could use another pair of strong hands."

"I'm happy to come help," I reply. "I'll be here at the lab for another few hours and then I can sneak out for the rest of the weekend."

"Fantastic. I'll see you soon then. Be safe. Love you."

"Love you."

I hang up and blow out a gusty breath. With the Halloween street party happening tomorrow, that means All Hallows' Eve is the day after, and we'll be preparing for our Samhain ritual in the bayou, in a field not far from Miss Sophia's cottage. Something tells me that that ritual won't go as planned. I'm not a fortune teller, and I can't see the future, but as the days progress, I've felt an urgency slowly building, as if I can sense that something is about to happen. It doesn't take a rocket scientist to figure out that it's something to do with Horace.

He's escalating. We know now that he's been ramping up for decades, killing dozens of people over the course of his adult life—and even now that he's dead. His spirit is strong. To my knowledge, he's never been able to continue killing past death, though.

But in this lifetime, he was somehow able to learn and hone the dark magic that runs through his lineage. It shouldn't surprise me that he'd figure out how to carry on past the death of his physical body.

It's not long before the door of my office opens, and Miss Sophia walks in. She grins when she sees me and offers me her hand.

"It's lovely to see you, child," she says. "How can I help?"

"I want to show you the bloodstones from the murders and run some theories by you."

She nods once and then follows me into the lab, where the stones sit untouched on my bench.

"What have you learned?" she asks.

"That each one was covered in the blood of the same person," I reply. "And just today, before I called you, I learned that when I hold one with my bare hands, I get physically ill."

Her sharp eyes whip over to mine. "Fascinating. Have you not touched them with your bare hands before?"

"Only once, and I felt a little nauseated then, but I

always wear gloves. I took the gloves off and was pacing around the lab, trying to think. Then, I picked one up without realizing what I was doing and got violently ill from it. Once I settled down, I reached for another to test the theory, and had to set it down immediately because I felt like I was going to be sick again."

She blinks as she studies the stones. "I'm going to pick one up."

"I don't want it to hurt you."

She smiles softly. "I'm safe."

She picks up a stone and holds it in the palm of her hand, covering it with the other hand. She takes a deep breath and closes her eyes. A moment later, she sets it down again.

"It didn't shock you," I say. "And you don't look like you're about to be sick."

"No, I feel fine, but I did learn quite a bit."

"Tell me."

"The stones are a gift for Millicent."

"A gift she can't touch."

Miss Sophia nods. "Absolutely. As you know, a bloodstone is mainly for cleansing and protection. He's cast a strong spell on the stones, covering them in magic for Millicent. He doesn't want her to touch it because he doesn't want her to diminish the strength of the spell."

"He cast a spell on me to throw up?"

"Not exactly. He's determined to keep Millie safe *from* you. He wants you gone, Lucien. The spell is to keep Millie safe and to cast you aside."

"Yeah, well, good luck with that." I drag my hand down my face in agitation. "He should know after a millennia that I'm not going anywhere."

"I don't know how much he remembers," she says, thinking it over. "I know *you* remember, and that Millie is beginning to. But, Lucien, for all we know, Horace is a tortured soul, reborn over and over again with the desire to kill. To taunt. To hurt. He feels a driving need to do it. But maybe he's not even aware of the *why* of it all."

"If you expect me to feel sorry for him—"

"Not at all. I'm simply pointing out that you may be expecting too much from him. He knows that, in the here and now, you're standing in the way of something he wants with Millie. And he wants you gone. He's also using you as a tool to hurt her."

"Which only pisses me off more. What else did you see when you held the stone?"

"Only the spell," she says. "I can't see where he cast it. Whether he remembers previous encounters or not, he's incredibly strong and gifted at his sick craft, Lucien."

"I know. And I feel as if something's coming soon."

She smiles like a proud mother. "Because you're strong and gifted, as well."

"I've done nothing but study for this since I was old enough to read," I remind her. "And yet, I still don't feel ready."

"You will be, when the time is right. But if the six aren't together in the end, it will all be for nothing."

Another reason to feel frustrated. "I know. We're working on that. Daphne is a stubborn woman."

"Like her sisters. She has to come to terms with her feelings on her own. She can't be forced. If the six aren't assembled of their own free will, coming together with pure love and peace, it won't work."

I nod and then pull the small woman in for a hug. Miss Sophia has always made me feel loved, as if I'm a member of her family. "For being so little, you sure are a powerful thing."

"What a lovely thing to say." She laughs and pats my chest. "I have other things to tell you, things you need to know, but I can't share them until I have you and Millie together. Come to my cottage tomorrow for lunch?"

"We would love to, but she's preparing for a Halloween street party in front of the café tomorrow night. I don't mind that this is taking all of her attention right now. She needs something happy, and this street fair is the perfect distraction. She goes all out, and it's her favorite day of the year. She's like a kid on Christmas morning. She's always loved Halloween."

"Even before?" Miss Sophia asks.

"Always."

"You're going to wear this tomorrow night."

Millie's holding a red devil costume on a hanger.

"Uh, no. I'm not."

"You *have* to," she says. "Brielle, Daphne, and I are going as the Sanderson Sisters. You know, from the movie *Hocus Pocus*? And we need you to be Master. It's hilarious. You remember that movie, right?"

"I don't know that I've had the pleasure."

"Oh, we're watching it tonight then. Gary Marshall plays this guy just dressed up as the devil for Halloween, and the sisters think he's the *real* devil, so they call him Master. It's a hoot and a half."

"Did you just say *hoot and a half*?" I tap her nose with my finger, delighted with her.

"Seriously, you have to do it. Or, I guess Cash can wear it, and we'll call *him* Master."

I narrow my eyes on her and lean in to whisper in her ear so those around us, who are currently helping us set up for tomorrow night, don't overhear. "You'll call no one Master in this, or any other life, *a stór mo chroí.*"

"It's just for fun."

I blow out a breath. "Fine. I'll wear the damn thing."

"Awesome." She smacks a kiss on my cheek and then hurries off to see to the lights being strung over the street.

"You're good for her," Brielle says as she joins me. "And you make her happy."

"That's my only goal." I glance down at her. "Is this

where you do the big sister thing and threaten to kill me if I hurt her feelings?"

"No, that goes without saying." She waves me off. "This is where I do the big sister thing and ask you to not only make her happy, but also keep her safe."

She holds my hand in hers and looks up at me with intense blue eyes.

"I've seen what he's capable of. I've felt his wrath. And for a moment, I thought I'd be lost to him. I couldn't bear it if—"

"I'll keep her safe," I promise. "Our strength grows every day."

"Something's coming," she says and swallows hard as she looks over to where Millie's laughing with Dahlia as they make flower arrangements together. "I feel it in the air. And early this morning, there was blood on the moon."

A shiver runs down my spine. "It's just a haze in the sky, Brielle."

"You and I both know that's not true." She pulls her hand out of mine just as Cash approaches.

"Dude, you have your own girl. Stop trying to flirt with mine."

"I swear, it was innocent."

"Sure." He winks at me and then smiles down at his wife. "How are you today?"

"Just fine. I'm glad you're here to help. We need to move the Jack-o-lanterns out onto the sidewalks."

"You do realize they'll be vandalized and ruined by tomorrow morning."

"You're such a cynic," Brielle says, rolling her eyes. "Of course, they won't be, because Millie's going to cast a little spell to avoid such a thing."

"*Of course*, she is. Why didn't I think of that?"

The two wander off, and I glance over to Millie. She's concentrating on a bouquet of black roses in her hands. She pricks her finger on one of the stems and immediately puts the tip of the digit into her mouth. Her eyes find mine.

Let's talk. I mouth the words. She nods, says something to Dahlia, and then hurries over to me.

"What's up?"

"I want to go inside where it's quieter," I whisper, and with her hand linked to mine, I lead her into her café and back to her small office. "We didn't cast the spell to open our door yesterday."

"I guess the day got away from me," she says. "Do you want to do it now?"

"Yes. And here's the thing, Millicent. We can close it after all is said and done and we're past this little war. Or, we can keep it open for the rest of our lives. It's completely up to you."

"Can we read each other's thoughts?"

"No." I brush my thumb under her left eye, sweeping away an eyelash. "We can simply talk to each other whenever we want, except we don't have to worry about a cell signal."

"Well, I like the sound of that." She grins and leans against me. "Thank you for doing this."

"It's for me as much as it is for you. I also want you to stick close to me for the foreseeable future."

She frowns up at me. "What's wrong? I mean, aside from the obvious. Has something changed?"

"I don't have anything concrete to tell you, but I have a bad feeling. I'm going to stick close to you, and I want to keep the door open at all times."

She shivers as she nods. "Done."

We join hands, and I begin to chant to cast the spell.

Light of day, and dark of night,
Find my soulmate in spell's flight.
Mind to mind, and heart to heart,
Connect us now while we're apart.
From this day, 'til we decree,
Make us one, so mote it be.

A breeze blows around us as the words are said. Millie joins in, chanting the words with me. When we're finished, we open our eyes and look at each other.

I love you, Millicent.

She smiles and presses her cheek against my chest, holding on tightly. *I love you, too, beloved.*

CHAPTER TWENTY-ONE

Millie

"I smell children!" Brielle, dressed as Mary Sanderson, startles a group of kids who gathered at my booth for some hot chocolate. They giggle and shriek in joy.

"We *are* children," one of them says with a laugh.

My sisters and I take Halloween *very* seriously. Every year, we dress up as famous witches, and this year, the Sandersons are in the rotation. Brielle's dark hair is teased up, and she twists her jaw to the side to make herself look like the character from the movie. I'm Sarah tonight, with my long, blond hair teased, and my dress showing off my cleavage. Once in a while, I break out in, "*Amok amok amok!*" and make everyone around me laugh.

"Sisters!" Daphne exclaims as she approaches the booth—well enough to make Bette Midler herself proud. "It seems there are children about."

"It's Halloween," a little Tinker Bell informs her. "Of course, there are children."

"Did you know we *eat* little children?" Daphne asks as she leans down to eye-level with the little girl.

"We don't really," I insist as I pass the child her little cup of hot chocolate. "Stop scaring away my customers, Daph."

"You know Halloween is my favorite," she replies, not sorry at all. She pats her red hair and gives me a toothy grin, thanks to her prosthetic front teeth. "I'm totally in character. I'm gonna go make the rounds."

"Have fun," I reply as I wave her off. This is the *best* night of the year. The street looks fantastic, if I do say so myself, with the orange lights strung back and forth over the street. The Jack-o-lanterns are lit and grinning, thanks to Lucien's handiwork. Each booth has a bouquet of black roses, thanks to Dahlia, and I love that folks feel safe to bring their little ones out here to trick-or-treat and enjoy the fun.

"I want some caramel corn," Esme says as she passes out another free hot chocolate. "And then I'm gonna man this station for a while so you can go mingle."

"We'll take turns," I assure her. "And you look adorable tonight, by the way."

She smiles and adjusts her black ears. "Meow."

"You make a sexy black cat in that suit."

"Thanks. It's not fun when I have to go to the bathroom, but it shows off my curves pretty nicely, if I do say so myself. Maybe I'll find a date tonight," she replies and crosses her fingers. "A girl can hope."

She hurries off to get her popcorn. I have a table set up just inside the café door for tarot readings, and Gwyneth is manning the counter inside so parents can order coffees, along with some special potions. I offered to help her, but Gwyneth insisted that she could handle it.

She's a fast learner, and a delight to have around. I hope she'll want to stay for a long while, even if it's just one day a week.

"How's it going?" Lucien asks as he sidles up next to me and kisses my temple.

"You're not wearing your costume."

He sighs with exasperation. "Do you know how tight that thing is? It left nothing to the imagination. I'm not wearing it."

"But you're not dressed as *anything*."

"I'm a scientist," he reminds me. "So, I'm dressed as a scientist."

"If we had a khaki jacket, you could mess up your hair a bit and look like Egon from *Ghostbusters*. A much sexier version, of course."

"No thanks."

"Killjoy."

Lucien laughs and tugs me against him for a long, slow kiss that makes my toes curl, and the candles in the Jack-o-lanterns burn a little brighter.

"There are children about," I remind him.

"And I don't care." He flashes a cocky smile. He leans in to whisper in my ear. "I can't wait to get you home and have my way with you."

"Just hold that thought for a few hours."

"I'll suffer," he says with a deep sigh, then offers me a wink and starts ladling hot chocolate into little cups. "But I think I can survive a few more hours."

"Can I steal her away?" Dahlia asks as she skips up to the table. Everyone is just so *happy* tonight. I absolutely love it. "I mean, I know I'm interrupting a romantic moment and all, but we haven't been down to the Head Over Heels booth to check out the shoes yet. And Mama needs some new kicks."

"Oh, yes, I want to look at shoes." I look up at Lucien. "Can you handle this for a bit?"

"Sure, have fun." *Stay close by.*

I'm just going down the street.

He winks, and Dahlia and I set off down the block.

"You outdid yourself this year," Dahlia says. "The music, the fog. How did you do the fog, by the way?"

"Little fog machines, strategically placed," I reply with a satisfied smile.

"Well, it's fun. And maybe a little creepy, but not over-the-top, so it's perfect for the kids."

"That's exactly what I was going for," I say. "Also, you're the cutest Wednesday Adams ever. I love the wig."

She grins happily. "Thanks. I've always liked Wednesday. Oh, here we are. Hi, Charly."

"Well, hello ladies." Charly gives us a welcoming grin. "It's been a minute since I've seen either of you."

"I know, I need to come in more often. I need shoes like crazy, and I just miss you."

Charly and I have owned our shops for about the same amount of time, and we became fast friends. Her brother is married to Mallory.

"Well, I have some *fabulous* new things on display, but nothing is for sale here. If you want something, you have to go down to the shop. I'm mostly here for exposure and to pass out candy. Oh, and to show off my costume, of course."

Her dress is *huge*. And sparkly.

And she's holding a wand.

"You're Glinda the Good Witch."

"That's me, sugar," she says with a wink. "I'm a hit with the little girls."

"Oh, I'm sure you are." I laugh and pick up a pair of black flats. "These would be great for work. Is it possible for you to call the shop and ask them to hold a size seven? I'll pick them up tomorrow."

"Sure thing," Charly agrees.

"Look at these," Dahlia says, holding up a pair of red stilettos. "The heel is so pointy. You could just drive it right into a man's heart."

I scrunch up my nose. "What in the world is wrong with you? That's disgusting."

"Oh, come on, it's Halloween."

"You need to lay off the horror movies, friend."

"No way, it's the perfect time of year for them." She giggles. "And I wonder why I'm single."

"Yeah, that's not really a great pickup line. '*Hey, handsome. Do you like my shoes? They're pointy enough to drive into your heart.*'"

We laugh and admire the rest of the shoes. I put one more pair, some black heels, on hold, and then we make our way back to our own booths.

"You should read my tarot cards," she says.

"I can totally do that. But don't you have to man your own stuff over there?"

"My staff has it under control for now."

"Well, let's do it then."

"But let's do it outside," Dahlia suggests. "I love the commotion of all the kids and the fresh air. It's a nice night."

"I like that idea. We can keep an eye on things. I'll grab my deck and be right out."

I hurry inside, grab my cards, check in with Gwyneth—who just shoos me out of the way—and when I decide that everything is under control, I return to Dahlia.

We sit at a table in my booth, and I ask her to cut the deck.

Esme and Lucien are behind me, passing out hot chocolate and admiring costumes.

Everything okay? Lucien asks.

Having a great time, I assure him.

"Okay, let's get started." I start, laying the cards on

the table. I frown. They're not making any sense at all. "Are you sure you cut the cards *exactly* where you wanted to?"

"I did," she says.

"Huh." I place a few more on the table in the spread. "I've honestly never seen this before."

"What is it? What do they say?"

"That's just it, Dahlia. They don't say *anything*. They're jumbled and don't make any sense at all."

"Sounds like my life." She snorts. "Makes perfect sense to me."

"You need to recharge your stones," I begin, all serious now. "You need to meditate and realign your chakras. Smudge your home and your store. I'm serious, Dahlia, you might think this is funny, but it's not good. And it explains a lot. Your clumsiness, for example."

"I have been extra clumsy lately," she says with a nod. "You're right. Maybe I've just felt overwhelmed lately. I haven't taken the time to reset and recharge."

"Are you okay? I haven't seen much of you, and you just haven't been yourself."

"I know." She blows out a breath. "Listen, tonight is for *fun*. So let's not worry about this right now. I'm doing okay, and now that this is in the forefront of my mind, I can focus on myself a bit over the coming days. The ritual with the blue moon the day after tomorrow will help."

"Oh, you're *so* right. That will be amazing for you. For all of us, really. Good thinking."

Dahlia pats my hand and then leaves to check on her booth.

"I'm worried about her," I say to Lucien as I join him by the hot chocolate.

"I have been, too. I've just been a little busy with other things. After the hunter's moon rite, I'll have a sit-down talk with her."

"Good idea."

"Hey, guys, lookie here. Hot chocolate for all the babies."

A group of four teenagers approaches our booth, all with arrogant little sneers on their acne-filled faces.

"Does that mean you'd like a cup?" I ask innocently.

The friends laugh, but the boy, the *leader,* doesn't think it's funny and knocks a stack of cups over.

"You can be on your way," Lucien says, his voice hard but low.

"Or what?" the boy asks. "What will you do about it? Sic your little witch on me?"

I smile and pick up a black candle. Lucien snaps his fingers, and the wick ignites, making the kids' mouths fall open, and their eyes bulge.

"Nice trick." The boy swallows hard. "It's just a little parlor trick you probably learned on YouTube."

I raise a brow, waggle my fingers, and conjure the wind to blow through their hair and then extinguish the flame.

"Whatever, freaks."

"You know," I say as I calmly set the candle down,

"we were taught to be more respectful, *kinder* to others. Wouldn't it be a shame if you and your little buddies here all turned into little black kittens tonight in your beds?"

He starts to smirk, but I snap my fingers and a black cat jumps onto the table, then sits and begins cleaning himself.

"Sorry, ma'am," the boy stammers.

"Just *enjoy* the street party," I suggest. "And stop trying to ruin it for everyone else. Would you like some hot chocolate?"

"No thanks." All four of them shake their heads and hurry away.

"Okay, where did the cat come from?" Lucien asks.

I snap my fingers again, and it's just Sanguine, staring at me as if to say, *really?*

"Good one, my love," Lucien says.

"Amok amok amok!" I bounce on my heels. Brielle hauls off and sticks her elbow in my stomach. "Ooof."

"You guys crack me up." Esme tosses used cups into the trash. The party is over, and we're finishing up with tidying the café before we all go home for the night and sleep like the dead. "And if I laugh any more, I'm going to pee my pants. I've been holding it because wiggling out of this bodysuit is a chore and a half, but I'm afraid I can't anymore. Be right back."

She runs toward the bathroom, making us all chuckle.

"I like her so much," Gwyneth says. "She's helpful and sweet. And such a good witch."

"She *is* talented," I agree. "Oh, Daph and B, I keep meaning to talk to you, but also keep forgetting. Our coven is performing an All Hallows' Eve ritual the day after tomorrow, and I want you to come."

"Us?" Brielle asks.

"Yes. You've never been before, and I think you'll really love it. It's beautiful. You can just watch."

"Are you going to be dancing naked under the blue moon?" Daphne asks.

"No—"

"Yes," Lucien and I reply at the same time. I bump him with my hip.

"No," I repeat. "But I'll dance for you naked after."

"If everyone keeps their clothes on, I'm in," Brielle says. "I think it'll be fun to watch, and the members of your coven have been nothing but accepting and protective of us. How can we not support this? It's like Christmas for you."

"Oh, I'm even *more* excited now."

Gwyneth sighs as she tosses her used towel into the hamper under the sink. "I think that's all of it back here, boss."

"You were an amazing help tonight," I say. "I'm so grateful you were here. Thank you for everything."

"It's my pleasure, honey. I'm going to head home and

see what kind of trouble Aiden got into while I was gone."

"Have a great night."

"I'll walk you to your car." Lucien squeezes my hand. "I'll be right back."

Lucien escorts his mom out the front door.

"Okay," Daphne says as soon as the door closes. "Now that he's not within earshot, I can say this. I *love* him, Mill. He's so nice, and smart, and the way he looks at you is just...gah."

"He's the best," Brielle agrees.

"Hey," Cash says, looking up from his phone. He's been in the corner, checking in with his team. He arrived late because of an investigation that ran long. He looks exhausted.

I know he's been working hard on our case, and that ours isn't the only one on his plate.

"I mean, he's the best for *Millie*." Brielle walks over and plants a kiss on her husband's lips, sans prosthetic teeth. "No one's better for me than you, babe."

"That's right."

"Thanks, guys," I say with a happy sigh. "I'm so mad at myself for fighting the attraction for so long. Because he's *amazing*. I could have been having the best sex ever all this time."

"That is a bummer," Daphne adds. "But it happened when the time was right. I'm really happy for you."

"Don't make me cry," I say, pointing to my sisters.

"Now, I'd better take this trash out so we can all go home."

"I can do it," Cash offers, but I wave him off just as Lucien walks back into the café.

"No, I'm fine. It's not heavy. I'll be right back."

I can hear Esme struggling to get back into her catsuit as I pass the restroom.

"Come on, you son of a bitch."

"You okay in there?"

"Do you have a crowbar?"

"No, ma'am."

"Then I'm okay. I just might have to go home half-naked."

I laugh and continue through the reading room to the back door. It's pretty dark back here, but I don't bother to turn on the light.

I know my way around like I know my own reflection.

I open the door, and just as I step out, my foot catches on something and I pitch forward, falling flat on my face.

I shriek, then wince when I feel the scrapes on the heel of my hand.

"Damn it."

"Are you okay?" Esme asks as she hurries outside. "I just left the bathroom and heard you...oh, goddess."

"What?" I glance over and feel the blood leave my face. "Oh shit. LUCIEN! CASH!"

The words come out in a scream. I crab-crawl away

from the body on the ground just as the others come running outside.

"Motherfucker," Cash spits out, pissed as hell. "I was twenty yards away. He dumped this one right under my nose."

"Under all our noses," Lucien says as he steps gingerly around the corpse, careful not to touch anything, and helps me off the ground. "Are you hurt?"

"Just my hand." I show him the scrapes, and he lightly brushes his thumb over the flesh, leaving it as good as new when he's finished.

"How did you—?"

"Practice," he murmurs before kissing my forehead. "Lots of practice, *a stór mo chroí.*"

Cash is already on the phone to call for help.

Brielle and Daphne take the trash I brought outside to the dumpster.

Esme's standing by the door, watching with wide eyes.

"What's on your hand?" I ask her. It's red.

Blood red.

My goddess, is Esme possessed by Horace?

"Oh, it's food coloring," she says, waving me off. "From the hot chocolate."

I nod, but I'm not convinced. This body wasn't here earlier. Esme went to the bathroom, and when I came back here, I literally fell over a dead man.

Sirens fill the air, and I know we're in for a long night.

"You guys should go home," I say to my sisters and Esme.

"Not yet," Cash adds. "We're going to have to take statements. It won't be too bad because I was here."

"You couldn't have stopped this." Brielle takes his hand, trying to reason with him.

"It's my fucking job to stop this," he says, shaking his head. "Right under my damn nose. He's an arrogant son of a bitch."

CHAPTER TWENTY-TWO

Lucien

I t's imperative that I hide my grimoire. I feel him growing impatient, and I know the time approaches when we will have to fight him.

My wife is in bed with our daughter, Sabrina, snuggled up at her breast. The baby hasn't been feeling well, so Millie has been bringing her to our bed for comfort.

What she doesn't know is that having both of my girls with me brings me comfort, as well.

Tarot, Millie's familiar, is curled up at the end of the bed and opens one eye when I get up and walk across the room.

"Keep them safe," I whisper to her. "I'll be back."

I retrieve my book of spells, the one that's been handed down to me for generations, and carry it down the stairs and into the library.

There is no better place to hide a book than amongst hundreds of other books.

I climb the ladder and clear a row of leather-bound fiction

novels from the shelf, push on a panel, and grin when I see the hiding space open. I push my grimoire inside, then return the novels to their places, covering it up.

I ease my way down the ladder and head back up the stairs, where I see the girls haven't even moved. Tarot yawns in greeting, then spins in a circle and falls fast asleep.

I slip back between the covers and kiss the baby's head. Millie shifts and smiles at me in the glow of the one candle I lit when I awoke.

"Are you all right, beloved?"

"Of course. I was just checking on something."

She closes her eyes. Did you hide it?

I smile. Millicent and I don't have secrets. Yes. In the library.

Good.

I brush my thumb across her forehead and lie awake for a long while, watching them both sleep dreamlessly.

I wake slowly with the dream still at the forefront of my mind. I remember almost everything from my previous lifetimes, but this is a new revelation. I check on Millie, who's sleeping soundly next to me.

With the moon almost full, I don't need any additional light to see as I ease out of bed and pull on some shorts.

Sanguine is curled up at the foot of the bed and opens one eye.

"Keep her safe," I whisper as I silently walk out of the room and downstairs to the library.

I flip on the light and stare up. The bookshelves are

full of books. In my dream, I'd climbed up to the second shelf from the top.

"Let's give it a try," I murmur and roll the ladder to the right place, then climb. When I reach the right row, I start pulling down books. I quickly flip through them to make sure nothing has been stashed between the pages and then let them fall to the rug below. But when I've uncovered the entire shelf, there is no panel.

"Damn."

I know the dream was real. Maybe this room was remodeled since then, and the book I hid is long gone. I sigh and rub my hand over my face, and then pound my fist on the shelf in frustration.

A panel shifts.

Holy shit, it was painted over.

I push on it, and the panel opens. Inside is my grimoire.

I pull it out and descend the ladder, then sit in one of the chairs and open the cover.

1821 is written at the top of the page. I know that *I* was not born during that time, but my great-grandmother was. At least, my great-grandmother from that particular lifetime.

And she left this to me.

"What are you doing?" Millie asks from the doorway. Her eyes are heavy with sleep as she surveys the pile of books on the floor. "Rearranging?"

I lift my hand, and all of the books return to their places on the shelf.

"Well, isn't that handy? Can you clean the whole house like that? It'll save some time."

I smile as she pads into the room and sits in the chair next to mine.

"Is that mine?"

"No, it's mine."

She frowns. "I didn't know you had a book of shadows."

"Neither did I until about thirty minutes ago." I tell her about the dream, and coming down here to look. "It's always a bit jarring when I discover something new."

"You can't possibly remember every single moment," she points out. "It makes sense that things come back to you here and there. That's a beautiful grimoire."

"My great-grandmother wrote it. Well, Lucien's great-grandmother from a hundred years ago anyway."

"And she gave it to you?"

"Yes, before she passed away. I was close to her. Learned a lot from her. Miss Sophia reminds me of her in many ways. She was patient and seemed to know everything. I always wondered how she literally knows all of the answers."

"Because she'd lived a full life, and you were a young boy," Millie says with a gentle smile. "I think it's lovely that you were close to her."

"I know there might be stuff in here that can help us." I offer her an apologetic grin. "I know, more reading."

"It will be fascinating," she says. "This is priceless, Lucien. You should think about putting a spell on it so it can't be stolen or destroyed."

"I already considered that. I'll do it in the morning."

I set the book on the side table and reach for my wife, then pull her into my lap. She drags her fingertips down my cheek before offering me her sweet lips. With my mouth pressed to hers, I snap my fingers, and the lights go out.

"I wonder what it's like," I murmur as my lips trail down her neck, "to have sex in a library."

"I think we're about to find out."

***

"I WONDER what Miss Sophia wants to talk about," Millie says the next morning as we buckle our seatbelts and leave the house. "I hate it when she's vague. It could literally be *anything*."

"If it was an emergency, she would have said so," I remind her and kiss her hand. "Before we head out to the bayou, I need to stop and talk to Cash."

"Okay."

One of the things I love most about Millicent is how easygoing she is. Not much ruffles her feathers. She's openminded and patient, two things I admire.

I make a turn and park in front of the police station, but rather that having to go inside, I see Cash waiting on the front steps.

"I have the newest bloodstone for you," he says and passes it to me. "I don't think you'll find anything different from the others, but it doesn't hurt to look."

"Agreed." I nod. "What else do we know?"

"The victim's throat was cut. There was no torture with this one, but the blood was pretty much drained."

I narrow my eyes. "Accident?"

"That, or necessity. I'm not sure. Who knows with this asshole?"

"Well, that's true. I'll take this to the lab and work on it later today."

"Sounds good. I'll let you know when and if I know more. We've decided to send in some of our cops who look a little like you, to the bars to try to lure him out."

I stare at the other man that I've come to consider my friend in such a short time. "That's dangerous."

"They're seasoned officers. They can take care of themselves. I'll keep you posted on that, too."

"Okay. Thanks, Cash."

He nods and waves at Millie, who's waiting in the car.

"I'll see you tomorrow night as we all dance naked under the blue moon."

I laugh and pat him on the shoulder. "You only have to dance naked on your first visit. After that, you can wear whatever you want."

"For fuck's sake," he mutters. "The things we do for love."

I laugh again, with absolutely no intention of easing

his mind and telling him that the naked dancing is something only done in fiction.

It's fun to tease him, as I would a brother.

"See you tomorrow," I say and return to the car.

"Everything okay?" Millie asks as she waves goodbye to Cash.

"Aside from innocent men dying? Yes. Everything's okay. I don't want to keep this stone on me, so I'm going to drop it by the lab on our way."

"Okay."

"You're quite agreeable this morning, darlin'."

She shrugs a shoulder. "What's not to be agreeable about? I get to spend time with you, it's a lovely fall day, and I know my café is being taken good care of by Esme and Gwyneth. I don't have any complaints. Except..."

"Except?"

"Well, last night, when I tripped on the corpse's ankle."

"Yes, I would complain about tripping on a corpse, as well, now that you mention it."

"No. I mean, yes, but that's not it. Esme ran outside when I yelped, and her hand was covered in a red stain. She said it was food coloring from the hot chocolate, but it looked like a *bloodstain*. And I just couldn't help but wonder if Horace could be possessing *Esme*."

"And you're just now bringing this up to me?"

"Well, there was a body on the ground, and then the cops came, and it was so late when we got home, I collapsed into bed. Then we had fun in the library. There really hasn't been time to accuse my employee and friend of being possessed."

I blow out a breath and laugh. "Okay, first of all, I don't think it's Esme."

"Why do you say that?"

"Because we cast some pretty strong protection spells on your café, Millie. There's no way that Horace could enter the building, whether in spirit form or in a host body."

She chews her lip. "Yeah, that's true."

"And Esme was working all night. She was with us at the booth, and then helping us clean up."

"She went to the bathroom," she reminds me. "And when I walked past, I heard her struggling to get back into her catsuit."

"So she was *in* the bathroom doing what she said she was going to do." I take her hand and squeeze it. "Esme has been with us at Miss Sophia's, and has been trying to help. I really don't think she's the one to look at."

"Okay." She sighs deeply and shakes her head. "What you say makes sense. I just wish we could figure out *how* this is all happening."

"We will. We just need to do it before he has a chance to destroy us first."

"Yeah, that would be ideal." She laughs at me as I pull into the parking lot of the lab. "Because I plan to spend a *lot* more years with you, *a mhuirnín.*"

I grin over at her. "Likewise. I'll be right back, I'm just going to drop this off."

I hurry inside and place the stone in the safe with the others, then return to the car. Millie's staring down at her phone.

"I'm having a girls' night at our place tonight with my sisters," she informs me. "They haven't been over to see the house yet, and I want to cook for them."

"That sounds like fun."

"Oh, it's gonna be fun," she agrees. "Daphne's bringing some cocktails."

"Will they need a designated driver?"

"Probably."

"Well, it's handy that I know how to drive."

"It's damn convenient having you around," she says with a laugh. "But that means no cocktails for you."

"That's okay. I don't drink much. I'm too busy studying most of the time and need a clear head."

"Now that you mention it, whenever I've been around you, you always have your nose in a book."

"My whole life," I confirm.

"Why?"

"Because I've been preparing for this, darlin'. Everything that we're dealing with right now is what I've been studying for."

And I'm damn frustrated that I still don't feel like I know enough.

"You're pretty amazing." She smiles at me from the

passenger side seat as I drive us out of the city toward Miss Sophia's house.

Amazingly terrified.

She squeezes my hand.

No need to be. I'm right here.

CHAPTER TWENTY-THREE

"Don't play with the forces of evil."
-- Anna Pistova
The Witch of Vladimirovac

"Oh, this game is getting fun," he murmurs to himself as he leans against a tree on the other side of the street from the big house in the Garden District. He followed them here after the party in the French Quarter. He stood back and watched as Millie and Lucien put on their little show for the asshole teenagers.

Those boys need someone to teach them how to respect their elders. *The way my girls do,* he thinks to himself.

Millie's so much more talented than she gives

herself credit for. Way too gifted to spend her evenings showing off with little parlor tricks for ungrateful children. It was all he could do to stand there and watch and not rail at her to stop, to open her eyes and realize that she was born for so much more.

All she needs is for him to teach her. But she just won't listen.

They *never* listen.

But he takes a deep breath before he gets frustrated again. That doesn't help anything. No, he needs to keep his head about him so there are no more mistakes.

A light comes on in the house across the street. He narrows his eyes and watches as Lucien, wearing only shorts, walks into the library. He looks up, then reaches for the ladder and climbs it, above the level of the windows.

He wants to see what Lucien's up to, but he knows that getting closer might give him away.

"Just be patient," he reminds himself. It looks like books are falling from the ceiling, and then, a few moments later, Lucien climbs down the ladder with a volume in his hand and sits in the chair. "Up for some reading in the middle of the night."

Suddenly, a light comes on upstairs, and Horace grins.

She's awake.

His gut clenches at the thought of seeing her. More lights flick on as she makes her way downstairs.

Suddenly, she's standing in the doorway, talking to Lucien.

"Me," he murmurs. "You should be talking to *me*."

He watches as she sits next to the other man and then snarls when Lucien lifts her into his lap, and she kisses his mouth.

That little whore.

Lucien snaps his fingers, and all the lights in the house go dark, shutting him out.

But it's for the best.

He's been ignoring his toys all day.

"Now, Lucien, I was not pleased when I saw you kiss her tonight." His voice is clear and calm, as if he's having a conversation with the man over coffee. "That's not to say that I don't know what you've been doing with her. Certainly much more than kissing."

The toy whimpers on his workbench.

"I understand." Horace pats the toy on the shoulder. "You're a man. And Millie is a lovely girl. Why, she'd tempt a saint with that curvy body of hers. And those tits? The goddess herself molded them with her very own hands. Yes, she's a beauty. All of my girls are."

He reaches for his new favorite knife, scowling as he thinks back on the blade he loved before. The one that was driven into his side and ultimately killed him.

But that's revenge for another day.

"Now, I think we should just make sure you can't lust after my Millicent anymore."

Horace grips the toy's penis between his finger and thumb.

"Don't worry. It won't hurt for too long."

He smiles and slices, reveling in the screams of pain, in the blood. In the power.

No, it won't hurt for long.

CHAPTER TWENTY-FOUR

Millie

Miss Sophia's house is warm and inviting as we step inside. Lucien brought the grimoire he found in the library last night. I can't wait for Miss Sophia to see it.

She is going to geek out.

"Hello, sweet ones," she says as she kisses both our cheeks and leads us to the dining room. "I have hot tea and fresh beignets for you."

"Your beignets are almost as good as Café du Monde's." I sit and pour myself a cup of tea, and another for Lucien when he nods. "Thank you for inviting us. It's good to see you and chat with you without the distraction of so many other people around."

"I do enjoy having my coven family around," Miss Sophia says. "And I also enjoy my alone time with you.

Both of you. How are you holding up with everything going on?"

"I think we're frustrated and worried," I reply honestly. "At least, I am. But I also feel stronger and more prepared than I've ever been."

"As you should," she replies. "Now that you're joined again, you're incredibly strong. Certainly, a force to be reckoned with. I have two reasons for bringing you here today. The first is, I want to discuss Ruth with you, Millie."

I tilt my head. "My mom? Is she okay? I haven't heard from the hospital."

"She's doing wonderfully," Miss Sophia assures me. "That's not it at all. In fact, I've been visiting her almost every day."

I immediately feel guilty for not doing the same. "I should have been going to check on her after we banished the spirit from her, as well."

"You've been a little preoccupied," Miss Sophia says. "And your mother knows that. I've been visiting because Ruth mentioned a few weeks ago, when you were here with her, that she'd like to start practicing the craft again. So, I go, and we cast protection spells together. Nothing difficult, but as we all know, practice and consistency is key."

"She's casting spells?" Lucien asks.

"Absolutely. And her Power and strength is coming back beautifully. I still feel horrible that I didn't know for all of those years that she was a prisoner, and that I didn't help her sooner. This is the least I can do. And, Millie, your mom is flourishing more every day."

"Well, that's wonderful."

"I'd like to invite her to the ceremony tomorrow night."

I sit back and stare at Miss Sophia. "You want to take her out of the hospital? Do you think she's strong enough for that?"

"I do. You'll know when you see her. She's not the woman you saw even two weeks ago. She's certainly healthy enough to join us in the circle."

"Well, if you think it's okay, I'm for it," I agree, surprising even myself. "Brielle, Cash, and Daphne are coming, as well."

"Oh, how wonderful," Miss Sophia says. "That will strengthen your bond, and that will only increase your chances of winning this next battle. I think that's a great idea."

"I hadn't thought of that," I admit and turn to Lucien. "Did you?"

"Yes."

"Well, don't I feel silly?"

"You shouldn't," he assures me. "You have a lot on your mind, *a stór mo chroí*."

"I love hearing that term of endearment." Miss Sophia gives us a sappy smile. "Now that we have Ruth settled, there's another reason I asked you to come. I hope that when you hear this story, you won't be angry with me for not telling you sooner. I just didn't feel that the time was right."

"What is it?" Lucien asks.

"As you know, Lucien, I come from a long line of witches. They predate record, as far as I know. So, the craft is engrained in me. Was since the day I was born. My sister was the same, goddess rest her soul. She died because of her gifts years ago. Because we were taught to use what we were given. To use it for good."

"That's one of the things I admire about you," I admit.

"Millie, you mentioned that you're beginning to remember bits and pieces from your previous time here. Can you tell me about it?"

"Lucien and I were married and lived in New Orleans, in the home we live in now in the Garden District. He worked at the hospital. I don't know if I worked." I frown as I think about it. "I don't think so. Everything I've seen is from after we had the baby. Sabrina."

Miss Sophia looks at Lucien. "Is that how you remember it?"

"Of course."

She nods. "Good. You were part of the coven, even back then. And as you know, it's a small community. So, I'd heard your names mentioned throughout the years."

"Your family knew ours?" I ask. "This is fascinating."

"Oh, it's about to get even more interesting," Miss

Sophia replies. "It's not just that my family *knew* yours. It's that—"

"That you were ours," Lucien finishes for her.

"What?"

"Sabrina was my grandmother," Miss Sophia says gently.

I sit back in the chair and stare at the woman I've come to love so deeply in the past decade. All this time, I was working with my great-granddaughter?

"I—"

"It's okay," Miss Sophia says and covers my hand with hers. She reaches for Lucien's hand, as well. "I know this is surprising and confusing.

"Lucien, Gwyneth and Aiden, your parents, and their parents before them, have also been a part of the coven for as long as I can remember, and for as long as we have records."

"How could they have known when I was born, who I am?" he asks.

"They didn't," she says. "They loved the name Lucien and gave it to you. And then you began to grow, and the things you knew...well, let's just say that's not a coincidence. And then I met Millie as a young girl, and I knew what was happening. Millie, when you came to me as a teenager, so eager to learn, I was very happy because I knew then that destiny had been set into motion. No one thought you'd return so soon. But your bond was—*is*—incredibly strong. Your love, unshakable. When Lucien died, Millicent was distraught, just a shell of who she once was. And Lucien's family was happy to take Sabrina, to raise her in the coven and teach her. To ensure that she knew how much her parents cherished her."

"That's what I said in the letter," I whisper.

"There's a letter?" Miss Sophia asks.

I nod and reach for my bag. "I've been carrying it with me. I know I shouldn't, in case it gets ruined, but I just haven't been able to put it away."

I pass her the old paper, and Lucien and I watch as she reads it.

Miss Sophia is our grandchild.

I grasp onto his hand at the sound of his words in my head. *This is incredible.*

"Well," she says as she tenderly folds the letter. "Isn't that lovely?"

"We also have the handfasting cord from then, and are wearing the original wedding bands."

Her eyes fill with tears. "What a gift."

"I have Sabrina's baby shoes at home," I inform her. "And you're welcome to see them. But, Miss Sophia, can you tell us about her? When I realized I'd been here before, and that I'd had children in other lifetimes, I didn't really stop to wonder what'd happened to those children. Until Sabrina."

"It would make sense," she says. "You're living in the house that she was born in. And you're living in a time not far from the one in which you lived with her. In the grand scheme of things, it's as if it happened last week."

"Yes." I nod and wipe a tear from my cheek. "That's how it feels."

"She was a wonderful woman," Miss Sophia adds. "I was very close to her. She was funny and happy. Much like you, Millie."

I press my hand to my mouth and let the tears fall.

"She was the most talented witch I've ever known, even to this day. She just *knew*. She always had the answers."

I smile up at Lucien. "You just said that about your own great-grandmother this morning."

Miss Sophia's eyes sharpen. "Which one?"

"Well, it would have been Sabrina's great-great-grandmother."

"Esther?" Miss Sophia asks.

"That's right."

"Oh, I'd heard stories," she says with a small laugh. "To talk about people long dead with you is so refreshing. It's as if they're still here. Nanna, that's what I called Sabrina, often spoke of Esther's grimoire and wondered where it was."

Lucien and I exchange a look of surprise, and then he reaches into his briefcase and pulls the book out, setting it on the table as he smiles.

"I found it just this morning."

Miss Sophia gasps in shock and covers her mouth with her hands. "You're kidding."

I reach over and open the front cover. "It's two hundred years old."

"Oh my goddess," she whispers, lovingly running her hands over it. "This is my four-times-great-grandmother's grimoire."

"I suddenly feel really old," I say with a laugh.

"You're not," she replies. "You're a thirty-year-old woman. Our DNA won't match. Nothing links us biologically. It's all spiritual."

"It's fascinating," Lucien adds. "I can tell you that I don't think anything like this has happened in any of my other lifetimes."

"That doesn't surprise me," she says. "Your Power has grown stronger as time passed. Your link to each other became more powerful. From what I was told, your death was sudden and had nothing to do with Horace, but that evil was escalating, and you feared that he'd get to Millie. You needn't worry, because he did *not*."

"Thank the goddess," Lucien whispers.

"And now, here you are, back to live out your destiny again. May I keep this book to read through and study?"

"Of course," Lucien agrees. "It's why I brought it today. I spent some time with it this morning. There are some fun things in there. Esther was pretty funny."

"I can't wait to read it," she says. "Now, back to Sabrina. She married at twenty years old. A fine, upstanding gentleman from New Orleans named Charles Patterson. They had three children. Their youngest baby died at birth from a defect. That would have been around 1945 or so. I'm the eldest child of *her* eldest child. My mother's name was Millicent."

I shake my head, completely overwhelmed.

"I'm so happy we came here today," I whisper, and then my eyes snap to Miss Sophia's. "Do you have photos of her?"

"Of course." She grins and reaches over to the counter and passes us a photo album full of black and white pictures. "She was beautiful. She had red hair, and deep brown eyes."

I look to Lucien. We'd talked about this. *Everything I remember is true.*

Of course, it is.

I brush my finger over Sabrina's face and wish I'd lived long enough in that lifetime to know my daughter.

"Don't do that," Miss Sophia says. "Don't wish for it to be different. Because if it was, you wouldn't be here now with your man. If you'd lived longer without him, you most likely wouldn't have been reborn in this time, and none of this would be happening."

"It's hard not to wish for it," I admit. "But you're right. I'm so happy that she was happy. That she was loved and had a beautiful family."

"She did have those things," Miss Sophia agrees. "Her Charlie was devoted to her until his dying day. She lived a long, full life."

I nod and smile at the photo of Sabrina on her wedding day. "Good. That's good."

"Okay, I'm obsessed with this house," Brielle says as she walks inside ahead of Daphne. "This place is gorgeous."

"Thank you. I made you guys spaghetti tonight. I hope that's okay. Lucien and I were gone most of the day."

Learning about our long-lost daughter.

Talk about a weird day.

I was sad earlier, but now I feel at peace knowing that Sabrina led a happy life. It's still weird to know that Miss Sophia is my great-granddaughter, and it's something I have to chew on for a while.

I'm not ready to share it with my sisters. Not quite yet.

"I'm so hungry," Daphne whines. "I'll eat anything you've got. And I brought dirty martinis."

"I love me a dirty martini," Brielle says. "Where's Lucien?"

"He went into the lab for a while. He said he'd give us some alone time. He'll be back later to give you guys a ride home."

"Good, because Cash dropped us off." Brielle steals a piece of garlic bread. "Let's eat first, and then we need the full tour."

"You got it."

Dinner is quiet as we all shove the pasta and red

sauce into our mouths, eating like we haven't had a meal in a week.

"I guess we were hungry," I say as I stare at our empty plates.

"Yeah, I'm gonna have a second helping after the tour." Daphne pours vodka into a shaker and gives it a shake. "Let's take our martinis with us."

"Good plan," I say, then clink my glass to my sister's. "To new beginnings."

"And to sisters," Brielle toasts. "Okay, let's do this."

I show them around the first floor. They both about swallow their tongues when they see the library.

"Yeah, that was my reaction, too."

"It looks like the library from *Beauty and the Beast*," Brielle says. "I want to be Belle."

"Later, you can climb up there and I'll push you along, and you can sing the song," I assure her with a laugh. "Now, let's keep going."

I take them upstairs and show them the guest suites. "We're going to furnish all of these. Not that I ever have anyone visit, let alone *five* at once. But it'll be nice to have them. It seems silly to leave them empty."

"You can make one an office," Brielle suggests. "And maybe one can be a spell room or something. They don't all have to be guest rooms."

"That's true," I say, thinking it over. "I'll have to do some research."

"We need to go up here." Daphne lays her hand on

the knob of the door that leads to the attic. "This is important."

"What do you see?"

"I don't know yet." She opens the door, flips on the light, and leads us up the stairs. "It's empty."

"Yeah. Over there is the hole where I hid our things."

I turn on my phone's flashlight and shine the light into the hole.

"Nothing in there now," Brielle murmurs. We sit in a circle on the floor and set our empty glasses aside.

Daphne reaches out and touches the hiding hole. "Oh. Oh, Mill. It's so sad."

"What is?" Brielle asks.

"She was devastated when Lucien died. She pined for him. Wrote a letter to him, and hid everything in here."

I don't think I told them about the letter.

"Did you read it?" Daphne asks.

"Yeah. It's sad. Like, really sad."

Daphne grins. "But there's a lot of happiness in this house, too. You and Lucien had a lot of fun here. And still are."

"For sure." I turn to Brielle. "Do you see any shadows here?"

"I don't want to tell you," she admits. "I just want you to be happy here."

I narrow my eyes. "I'll be happy if I know the truth.

Come on, B, I don't want to lower my shields and look. You know it's too dangerous."

She blows out a breath. "That's not fair."

"Please, tell me."

She glances around the attic. "I don't see anyone up here. There was an old woman downstairs who kept following us around. Not in a creepy way; more in a nosy way. Like, *what are you doing in my house* kind of thing."

"Oh, great. I have a nosy old-lady ghost."

"She didn't follow us up here. I also heard a baby crying but that's stopped."

"Huh. That's weird. But I guess babies were probably born in this house at some point. It's almost two hundred years old."

"Probably," Daphne agrees. "I don't sense a baby."

"It could just be an echo," I suggest. "Not a conscious spirit, just an energetic moment in time that repeats."

"Absolutely," Brielle agrees. "And that's likely in this case. The only thing I've seen is the old-lady shadow. Which, honestly, isn't bad for a house this old."

"True. I guess I shouldn't complain. I'm glad you guys are here. And I'm *really* glad you're coming to the ceremony tomorrow."

"Cash thinks he has to dance naked," Brielle says, laughing behind her hand. "I haven't corrected him. Does that make me a bad wife?"

"No, that's hilarious." Daphne laughs. "Maybe I'll

mention it in the car on the way there. That I'm nervous about being naked in front of all those people."

"Poor Cash," I say, shaking my head. "He married into a family of tormentors."

"Eh, he loves it." Brielle shrugs. "And he gives as good as he gets."

"You have a point." I grin at my sister. "Do you think we can actually get him naked before he discovers it's all a hoax?"

"We can certainly try."

CHAPTER TWENTY-FIVE

Millie

The air is cool in our bedroom this morning. The day is finally here, my favorite day of the year.

All Hallows' Eve.

When the veil between the living and the dead is the thinnest.

And this year is particularly special, with not just a full moon, but a full blue hunter's moon.

It's as sacred as it gets, and I get to spend it with the man my soul is linked to, along with my sisters, the brother of my heart, and my coven.

I'm so dang excited, I can hardly contain myself.

But I take a deep breath, trying to stay calm and centered. It's early morning, and Lucien is still sleeping beside me. Which is unusual. The man hardly sleeps. I'm constantly waking to find him either gone or lying awake beside me.

And now that I think about it, it's usually *me* who

has trouble sleeping. Plagued with dreams, I never slept much.

Until Lucien came back into my life.

Is it because he brings such tranquility to my life that I'm able to relax and sleep peacefully? And is he *not* sleeping well because he's taking that on himself, the way he does my headaches with just the sweep of his thumb over my forehead?

I don't know, but I have a hunch that all of that is true.

This morning, he's resting peacefully. His dark lashes fall against his cheek, and his breathing is even and slow.

I've been worried about him. He mentioned the other day—yesterday?—that he's frightened. Lucien doesn't show fear often. He's so confident, so sure of himself. So hearing that he's afraid was startling.

But he's not alone.

I feel the evil creeping closer, and I'm not any closer than he is to finding a solution. But we're stronger together, and I trust that we'll meet the evil head-on and win.

There's no other choice.

"I can feel your giddiness from over here," he mumbles, not opening his eyes.

"It's my favorite day," I whisper to him and press a kiss to his bare shoulder. "And I'm excited to get started with preparations for the ritual and the feast. There's so much to do."

"It can wait," he says as he rolls to me and cups my face in his large hand. His eyes are heavy with sleep as they drop to my lips. "First thing's first."

I'm expecting the frenzy that usually comes with our lovemaking. The swirl of air and flames.

But this morning, the room is calm and cool, and Lucien is slow and methodical as his hands journey over my body, waking it up to a slow burn.

He rolls me onto my back and stares down at me lovingly. Lucien is an intense man, and having that intensity directed at me, especially in the bedroom, is at once thrilling and overwhelming.

He links his fingers with mine, and I feel a light breeze blow over us. He locks his lips with mine, and the wind picks up.

A shiver of pure Power runs down my spine.

But it's when his body joins with mine that the flames of the candles ignite around us. The room has gone from calm to powerful chaos at just the joining of our bodies and souls.

I sigh, and the wind swirls.

He moans, and the flames reach higher.

And with the crescendo of our bodies, the Power around us builds and then calms, until it's just the two of us, spent and in love.

And feeling more connected than ever.

"Is this your family's property?" I ask Lucien as he pulls into the small parking area of the farm where our coven celebrates our sabbats and holds our rituals and rites. "I mean, the Lucien from before? Is this where Sabrina grew up?"

"I do believe Miss Sophia mentioned that this property has been in her family for generations, so I think so," he says. "All this time, we were walking where she once walked."

"It's mind-blowing," I admit. "I think it's going to take me a while to process it all."

"You can take all the time you need," he assures me. "I feel the same way. I understand it, but accepting it isn't as easy."

"Well, if you understand it, you're light years ahead of me." I get out of the car and open the rear door to fetch the food I've prepared for the feast. We're not the first to arrive, and I smile when I see Cash pull in next to us with Brielle and Daphne. "Hi, guys! I'm so happy you're here."

"I brought pie," Daphne announces. "I didn't know what else to bring. But everyone loves pie, right?"

"I love pie." Cash grins.

"And we brought some cornbread," Brielle says.

"My mom's recipe," Cash adds.

"You guys didn't have to bring anything at all. I'm just happy you're here." Lucien takes the gumbo I prepared this morning from my hands. "This cornbread will go great with the gumbo."

"You made gumbo?" Brielle asks. "You know that's my favorite."

"I know. I did it on purpose. I'm grateful you guys came."

"Honestly, I've wanted to come before," Daphne adds, "I just didn't know if it was appropriate because I'm not a practicing witch."

"You're always welcome here, child," Miss Sophia says as she joins us. "We welcome everyone who wants to be here, so long as they come with an open heart and a clear mind."

She turns to me.

"Did you tell your sisters?"

"About Mama? Yes, I told them last night."

"Is she here?" Brielle asks.

"She is, and I just can't wait for you all to see her." Miss Sophia takes our hands and leads us past an old farmhouse, where a cousin of hers still lives, to a back yard covered with tents, tables and chairs.

This isn't where we perform the ritual. That's out farther in the field, and we'll head that way to set up after we finish preparing and chatting.

"My girls," Mama says with joy as she sees us walk around the house. She's dressed in a long, green dress that flows around her legs with sleeves that ruffle away from her elbows.

Her long, blond hair is down, and she's wearing amber around her neck for protection.

"It's so good to see you, Mama," I say and fold her into a hug. "You look wonderful."

"I *feel* wonderful." She smiles, accepting hugs from my sisters, and Cash and Lucien, as well. "I'm so happy you're all here. Look at this beautiful family that I have."

I have to blink away the tears. *This* woman is the person my sisters and I longed for all of our lives. I'm just so relieved that she's herself again, and we can work toward healing as a family.

"I've been studying with Sophia." She takes my hand and leads us to the tents, where the guys set down the food. "We must have cast a hundred protection spells over the past couple of weeks."

"That's good," I say. "You need them."

"I do, but I'm also feeling much stronger. I won't allow anything like that to happen again. I have the tools to protect myself."

She fiddles with the amber around her neck, then grins as if she just got an idea.

"In fact, I want to show you something."

Mama walks to a nearby table where a candle isn't lit yet. She leans over and blows on the wick, and it lights.

"Look at you," Brielle cheers. "That's so damn cool, Mama."

"I think so," Mama agrees.

"There you guys are," Esme says as she hurries over. "I snagged a ride with Gwyneth and Aiden after we closed up the café for the day. You were right, Millie, customers couldn't get enough of the special Blue Moon Mocha today."

"That's so fun." I laugh. "I'm glad they liked it."

"I told them there was a little added blood magic in them," she says with a wink, and I take a step back.

Blood magic?

Blood.

Esme's turned away from me and is talking with Mama, but now my hackles are raised.

Why would she say that?

Stop it, Lucien says.

Something is off with Esme. I'm not crazy. Why would she mention blood magic?

Because it's mystical and people eat that shit up with a spoon.

I don't reply, just nod and decide that I'll be keeping a closer eye on Esme this evening.

"Lucien and Millie, can I speak with you?" Miss Sophia asks. She leads us to a private space on the other side of the house and has two pouches in her hands. "I wanted to give these to you yesterday, but decided to charge them under the full moon last night first."

She passes us each one of the pouches.

When I open mine, I find a necklace with a Mother of Pearl pendant the size of a baby's fist.

"Sabrina gave me these, and I think you should have them. They were originally yours to begin with. The Mother of Pearl is for harmony. It stimulates intuition, imagination, and sensitivity. And it's a beautiful piece of jewelry."

I brush my thumb over the stone, then loop it around my neck to join my amethyst.

"Thank you so much."

Lucien opens his pouch and finds a dagger with different-colored stones in the hilt. Emerald, sapphire, amethyst, among others.

"Sabrina didn't know where this dagger came from, just that it was yours, Lucien."

"It's ancient," he says with a sigh and turns it over in his hands. "I need to do some research to be sure. Thank you, it's beautiful."

"You're welcome." She smiles at us both. "Blessed be."

When we return to the others, I see that more members of the coven have arrived. It's always so fun to see familiar faces, to chat with those I only see a couple of times a year.

All of these people came to help us last year when we defeated Horace in the bayou. They're our family.

"Hey, guys," Dahlia greets as she approaches. "I thought I'd never get out of the shop today."

"Well, you're just in time," I assure her. Dahlia's eyes fall on my new necklace.

"That's gorgeous," she says. "And new."

"It's actually old. Miss Sophia gave it to me."

"I love it." She smiles. "I need to get myself a talisman. I just haven't decided what I want."

"You can always try out different ones and then go with the one that feels the best."

"Good idea."

We've walk over to where Mama's sitting with my sisters and Cash.

"Can we sit here?" I ask.

"You can," Mama says and then turns cold eyes to Dahlia. "But she's not welcome here."

I frown and glance at Dahlia, who seems completely unfazed.

"Mama—"

"No, it's okay," Dahlia insists. "I need to go say hello to someone over there anyway."

She walks away, and I sit next to Lucien. "Mama, that was rude. Dahlia's my friend."

"You should *not* be friends with that woman," Mama replies. "Her soul is dark."

"She did work in dark magic for a long time, but she left that coven and is now working with Lucien," I reply. "She's one of us."

Mama just shakes her head, and I decide to leave it alone for now.

I look over and see that Dahlia is sitting with Esme and Lucien's parents at a table nearby. I'll have to apologize to her later.

Esme looks my way and offers me a smile. I wave at her and then turn my attention to the conversation going on around me.

I have a feeling Esme is the one we need to be worried about.

⁂

WITH NIGHT DESCENDING QUICKLY, we gather our tools and sacred items and walk as a group out to the field.

The moon is high, big and yellow. I feel the strength of it soaking into my skin, and I'm grateful.

When all of the candles are set out in a wide ring, and the black salt is poured, we form a circle inside and join hands.

Suddenly, Cash reaches for the buttons on his shirt.

I share a look with my sisters and have to press my lips together so I don't laugh out loud.

"What are you doing, child?" Miss Sophia asks.

"Isn't this where we dance naked under the moon?" Cash asks.

I can't contain the bubble of laughter that escapes. Daphne snorts.

Brielle cackles.

"I guess not," Cash mutters. "I hate all of you. And just remember, payback's a bitch."

"Language, child. This is a sacred space," Miss Sophia says, but her lips twitch with mirth.

Lucien's laughing next to me, and as the others catch on to our little joke and join in.

"Come on, Cash, you know it's funny," Miss Sophia's

granddaughter, Lena, says. "At least you didn't get naked."

He narrows his eyes at me in response, then shakes his head and laughs, as well.

We join hands again, each take a deep breath, and Miss Sophia begins speaking the words that will cast our circle, beginning our ritual.

To start the rite, each of us must enter into the circle with perfect love and perfect trust and affirm as much when asked. We must all have a clear heart and mind and be open to the deities.

Miss Sophia stops mid-sentence before she even asks the first person to confirm their intent and looks around the circle.

"What's wrong?" Lucien asks.

"Someone here doesn't have pure intentions," she says. "I can't cast the circle."

My eyes fly to Esme, who's directly across from me. "Do you have something you want to tell us?"

Miss Sophia shakes her head. "It's not Esme."

"Then who—?"

My eyes follow hers. She's staring at Dahlia.

CHAPTER TWENTY-SIX
Millie

D ahlia's lips turn up into a smug grin. "I didn't say anything."

Mama, who's standing between Brielle and me, clenches our hands and starts to chant a protection spell. Brielle listens to Mama's words and then joins in, following Mama's lead.

Daphne joins them, then Cash, and then the entire circle, one by one, begins to chant the spell.

Dahlia snarls and lunges to her left for Lucien's dagger, but the hilt burns the palm of her hand and she drops it.

"I'll kill you," she snarls at him. "I'll kill all of you."

Her body jerks, her eyes go wide, and energy pours out of her mouth. When she's empty, Dahlia falls to the earth, unconscious.

An older member of the coven hurries to tend to Dahlia as the rest of us join hands once more, and Miss

Sophia succeeds in closing the circle. The wind and light around us is strong, the flames of the candles soar.

And suddenly, right in the middle of the circle, Horace manifests himself.

I blink, certain I'm not seeing what my brain says I'm seeing.

Is that him? I ask.

This is the moment we were born for, a stór mo chroí. My eyes fly up to Lucien's.

His are not afraid.

They're angry.

"You think you're the only ones with parlor tricks?" Horace snarls and, with the flick of his wrist, sends debris flying at us. Stones and twigs, grass and dirt fly at everyone, but no one waivers in their steadfast chanting of the protection spells.

I drop my shields. I *have* to see everything that he might throw at us.

And just as I do, shadows pour in from all around us, coming from the swirling wind above. They surround Horace with their arms linking around him in some sort of horrific protection.

"Do you see—?" Brielle starts to ask, but I just nod emphatically.

"The shadows."

Put your damn shields back up, Millicent.

No, I have to be able to see what he's doing. I can't stop him if I'm blind.

Horace turns to me and smiles gleefully. "Did you

miss me, darling? Have you enjoyed the wonderful gifts I've left for you?"

Do not answer him. Do not engage with him.

Horace turns to Lucien as if he can hear our private conversation and snarls. "You think you can control her? You think I'd let you *have* her? You stupid mortal, she doesn't belong to you."

Lucien reaches into his pocket and pulls out our handfasting cord, then takes my hand, the cord locked between us.

"I am hers, and she is mine, our souls forever linked. Be gone from here, any who would see us harmed, back to the shadows you must slink."

The chanting around us is heightened, and they've changed to the spell they used last year at Horace's cabin. It cast him out once, surely it will do so again.

He's stronger, Lucien tells me. *We need another spell to layer with this one.*

I wrack my brain, trying to think of something stronger than this one, but I can't think with *him* staring at me. The shadows are screaming. The wind is chaos.

Close your eyes.

I follow Lucien's instructions.

You control the wind, Millicent.

He's right. I take a deep breath, then open my eyes and bring the wind high above all of us and watch as Horace's smile falls, and he stares at me in confusion. Then blow out my breath, and the wind whips through the center of the circle, sending the shadows

scrambling. Horace is knocked on his ass from the force
of it.

He climbs to his feet.

"This is all in vain," he begins, but Lucien snaps his
fingers and encircles Horace in a wall of flames. I add
the wind, and the flames grow higher, burn hotter until
Horace is completely engulfed.

He's not done, I warn Lucien.

"The sacred banishment spell," Miss Sophia yells.
Immediately, the coven switches from one spell to the
next, their chanting becoming louder and louder.

Horace screams in pain.

With our hands still linked over our rope, Lucien
and I begin our handfasting ceremony.

I don't know how we know to do this, the words just
begin pouring from us.

As this knot is tied, so are our lives now bound.

*Woven into this cord, imbued into its very fibers, are all our
hopes, our Power, and the promise of our present life together.*

Over and over again we chant, our voices growing
louder each time as the others recite the banishment
spell.

Horace howls in pain.

Suddenly, he evaporates and is carried into the night,
along with the smoke from Lucien's fire.

The shadows disappear.

The flames calm, and the wind stops.

We look back and forth between the members of
the coven, and Miss Sophia's shoulders relax in relief.

"He's gone," she says with a deep sigh. "For now. Until the six are assembled, he won't be gone for good."

She looks at Daphne, who nods solemnly.

"You know what to do, child."

Dahlia moans from her spot on the ground just behind us. Lucien kneels next to her.

"I'm so sorry," she whispers. "I'm so, so sorry."

"Hey, take it easy," Lucien says gently. Gwyneth appears with some water, and we take a moment to let Dahlia get her wits about her. She presses her hand to her forehead.

"He made me kill you." The tears start now. "He made me kill you over and over again. In horrible, disgusting ways. I couldn't stop him. I tried so hard, I even tried to leave notes, but he would erase them. He smashed my phone when I tried to make a note there."

"He was much stronger than you," Lucien assures her. "And I'm right here."

"All those men," she says. "Tortured and slaughtered. He's the devil."

"Yes," Lucien agrees. "He is."

"Oh my God," Dahlia says. "More men are being held. We have to save them."

"On it," Cash insists, pulling his phone out of his pocket. "Where is his hiding place?"

"I don't know the address," she admits. "But I can show you. It's not far from the Quarter."

"You need to rest," I say.

"I can rest when those men are safe," Dahlia insists. "Come on, I'll show you."

Cash takes her hand and leads her toward the house. "I'll call you when we're finished," he calls out over his shoulder, already in cop mode, ready to go save Horace's victims.

"We're still going to cast the ritual circle for the All Hallows' Eve ritual," Miss Sophia insists. "It will strengthen us all. We can't let him destroy what we came here to do."

As we form the circle once more, Mama pulls me in for a strong hug.

"I'm so proud of you," she says and frames my face in her hands. "Now, let's enjoy our celebration, shall we?"

I nod and take Lucien's hand.

We did it.

He brushes his thumb over my forehead.

Together.

CHAPTER TWENTY-SEVEN

Lucien

It's been three days since the night in the field, and I'm not sure if my hands have stopped shaking.

I was terrified for days, knowing that the evil was about to culminate, I just didn't know when or how.

And I certainly didn't expect it to be Dahlia that he used as a host.

I glance over at Millie, who's picking green beans in our garden.

"I just found something," she says with a frown. She looks adorable in her oversized coveralls and wide-brimmed hat to keep the sun off her delicate skin. "Like, not a green bean."

"What is it?" I lean over to have a look. "A coin?"

"It looks like a silver dollar," she says with delight. "It's from 1902."

"Must be mine, then."

She rolls her eyes and shakes her head. "Finder's keepers and all that."

She tucks the coin into her pocket and then returns to picking beans.

"Have you talked to Dahlia today?" she asks.

"No, but I spoke with her last night. Her blood matches, Millie."

Her head whips around to look at me. "Matches what?"

"The blood on the bloodstones. He was cutting Dahlia and coating the stones with her blood."

"Which is why I saw the cuts on her arm that day," Millie says and props her hands on her hips. "You know, you mentioned that with all of the protection spells we cast, there was no way that Horace would be able to go into Witches Brew, even with a host."

"You're right."

"And it occurred to me that Dahlia hasn't set foot in the Brew since the day I found the blood on the mirror in the bathroom. She came to the door but never went inside. Even the night of the Halloween street party, she suggested I read her cards outside."

"What did her cards say?"

Millie sighs. "Nothing. They were a mess. They didn't make sense at all."

"But knowing what we know now, that makes sense, after all."

"Oh, Lucien, I feel so bad. I should have *known*.

Dahlia was acting strangely, and I didn't see it. She had good excuses for everything. Instead, I blamed my *friend*."

"And you apologized."

"I don't deserve Esme. She accepted my apology so quickly and said that she would have suspected everyone around her, too. I'm going to give her a raise, and a week's vacation."

"You're sweet," I murmur and kiss the top of her head. "I know she'll appreciate that. We'll check in on Dahlia later today. Maybe tomorrow."

"Why did he target her?" she asks. "I've been trying to figure that out."

"Because of her history with the dark coven," I reply. "He most likely knew her from that coven and remembered that she left. She would be vulnerable to possession."

"That's so messed up."

I tug her to me and hold her tightly, unable to hold off any longer.

"You've been a little clingy lately," she says. "Not that I'm complaining."

"It's relief," I admit. "I was so scared that I'd have to watch you die again. I just couldn't bear it, *a stór mo chroí*."

"Did you think we'd lose?" she asks in surprise.

"I didn't *know*, and that was the hardest part. I didn't know if we'd defeat him, or when he'd strike. I certainly wasn't expecting it to go down the way it did, but I'm grateful because we had an army of people on our side."

"I suspected it would happen there," she admits.

"Really?"

"Yeah, because I still suspected Esme. But also because he likes to show off, Lucien. He likes an audience. And what better audience than a circle of witches?"

"Very true. I'm sure he's pissed that he failed."

"He'll try again."

"Yes." I sigh and bury my lips in her hair. "He will."

"My baby sister needs to get her shit together, or we *will* lose again."

"She will," I reply with confidence. "I have faith in her. You need to, as well."

"Yeah, well, I believe in her. I also believe in the power of Brielle's nagging. She'll badger the poor girl into being with Jackson if it's the last thing she does."

I laugh and drag my thumb over her forehead. No headache today.

"Unfortunately, that's not how it works. She can't be nagged into it. It has to happen of their own free will."

"Then we might be doomed." Millie grins. "Does this mean we get to grow old together, *a mhuirnín?*"

"It means we're one step closer. I honestly don't know what happens from here. We've never gotten this far before."

"Wow," she breathes. "No pressure or anything."

I grin and tip up her chin so I can kiss her sweet lips. The love I have for this woman brings me to my knees. My chest aches with it. And I'll do everything in my power to keep her and those we love safe.

"No pressure at all."

EPILOGUE

Daphne

Six Months Later...

The wedding was absolutely stunning. Millie was radiant in her long, flowy white dress. We talked her out of wearing the one she wore a hundred years ago. I still can't believe she found it in a trunk in one of the empty bedrooms.

The whole *something old* is fine, but sometimes you need something new, for a fresh start. And this dress with its little forget-me-nots embroidered in the veil was just the right thing. And when Lucien saw her for the first time, well, let's just say there wasn't a dry eye in the field.

We're back in the same place we held the Halloween ritual, but I was relieved to see that all remnants of that scary night were swept away with cleansing spells and magic.

Thank the goddess for magic.

I've always left that sort of thing up to Millie. It's not that I don't believe. It's the exact opposite, actually.

It's that I've seen what magic can do, how it can destroy, and I avoid it like the plague.

Just like I avoid Jackson Pruitt.

Who, by the way, is *here*. And that's why I'm in the damn bathroom. I was so mad when Millie told me she invited him.

But he's her friend, and she's stubborn.

And I can handle it. I'm an adult. And I know that sooner or later—okay, sooner—we'll have to work together. I feel it.

I know he's part of my destiny.

But damn it, I'm just not ready. Not yet.

So, today, I'm going to pull up my big-girl panties and enjoy my sister's special day. I'll deal with Jack some other time.

I nod, happy with this decision and feeling bolstered from my little pep talk, and walk out of the bathroom.

It's suddenly grown quiet outside, which is odd for a wedding reception of at least a hundred guests.

I frown as I walk around the side of the house. The air is still. There's no music. No laughter or talking.

Just...*silence*.

"Hey, guys?" I call out. "What's going on?"

Everyone is standing, facing away from me. Not moving. Just standing as if they're in a trance.

"Guys?"

Collectively, they all turn to stare right at me.

And every single one of them is missing their eyes.

ABOUT SERENDIPITY

Coming October 2021!

From *New York Times* Bestselling Author, Kristen Proby, comes Serendipity, the final installment in her gripping Bayou Magic series...

I'm not a practicing witch, but there's never been any denying my oddities. At least I can put my psychometry to good use at my antique store—I mean, who wouldn't want to buy from someone who can see the history of every piece?

My gift, however, is also a curse. It cost me the love of my life. Sure, we were young, but some things you can't get over. Like being the cause of the biggest tragedy of your boyfriend's life. It's something I'll never forget, and a reflection of who I am.

But now that Jackson's back in town, medal of honor on his lapel, and scars aplenty. It's time for me to be brave, too. A malevolent evil hell-bent on making my sisters and me pay for rebuffing him is still stalking my family, and some ancient writings portended that *the six* were the only ones who could defeat him.

Apparently, Jackson Pruitt and I round out that magical number, which means I have to face him and the things he makes me feel, to save my family and my city.

I never sought to reconnect with Jack. His heart may be the most valuable thing I've ever touched or held. Working with him now means opening myself up to my feelings for him.

Refusing means destruction for us all.

For more information, visit: www. kristenprobyauthor.com/serendipity

ABOUT THE AUTHOR

Kristen Proby has published close to fifty titles, many of which have hit the USA Today, New York Times and Wall Street Journal Bestsellers lists. She continues to self publish, best known for her With Me In Seattle and Boudreaux series, and is also proud to work with William Morrow, a division of HarperCollins, with the Fusion and Romancing Manhattan Series.

Kristen and her husband, John, make their home in her hometown of Whitefish, Montana with their two cats and dog.

facebook.com/booksbykristenproby
instagram.com/kristenproby
bookbub.com/profile/kristen-proby
goodreads.com/kristenproby

NEWSLETTER SIGN UP

I hope you enjoyed reading this story as much as I enjoyed writing it! For upcoming book news, be sure to join my newsletter! I promise I will only send you news-filled mail, and none of the spam. You can sign up here:

https://mailchi.mp/kristenproby.com/ newsletter-sign-up

ALSO BY KRISTEN PROBY:

Dream With Me
You Belong With Me
Imagine With Me
Shine With Me

Check out the full series here: https://www.
kristenprobyauthor.com/with-me-in-seattle

The Big Sky Universe

Love Under the Big Sky
Loving Cara
Seducing Lauren
Falling for Jillian
Saving Grace

The Big Sky
Charming Hannah
Kissing Jenna
Waiting for Willa
Soaring With Fallon

Big Sky Royal
Enchanting Sebastian
Enticing Liam
Taunting Callum

Check out the full Big Sky universe here: https://
www.kristenprobyauthor.com/under-the-big-sky

Bayou Magic

Shadows

Spells

Check out the full series here: https://www.
kristenprobyauthor.com/bayou-magic

The Romancing Manhattan Series

All the Way

All it Takes

After All

Check out the full series here: https://www.
kristenprobyauthor.com/romancing-manhattan

The Boudreaux Series

Easy Love

Easy Charm

Easy Melody

Easy Kisses

Easy Magic

Easy Fortune

Easy Nights

Check out the full series here: https://www.
kristenprobyauthor.com/boudreaux

The Fusion Series

Listen to Me
Close to You
Blush for Me
The Beauty of Us
Savor You

Check out the full series here: https://www.
kristenprobyauthor.com/fusion

From 1001 Dark Nights

Easy With You
Easy For Keeps
No Reservations
Tempting Brooke
Wonder With Me

Coming in 2020:
Shine With Me

Kristen Proby's Crossover Collection

Soaring with Fallon, A Big Sky Novel

Wicked Force: A Wicked Horse Vegas/Big Sky Novella
By Sawyer Bennett

All Stars Fall: A Seaside Pictures/Big Sky Novella
By Rachel Van Dyken

Hold On: A Play On/Big Sky Novella
By Samantha Young

Worth Fighting For: A Warrior Fight Club/Big Sky
Novella
By Laura Kaye

Crazy Imperfect Love: A Dirty Dicks/Big Sky Novella
By K.L. Grayson

Nothing Without You: A Forever Yours/Big Sky Novella
By Monica Murphy

Check out the entire Crossover Collection here:
https://www.kristenprobyauthor.com/kristen-proby-crossover-collection

Made in the USA
Monee, IL
12 October 2020